created by

Stephen Hillenburg

rhcbooks.com

ISBN 978-0-593-12751-3

Printed in the United States of America

10 9 8 7 6 5 4 3 2

By David Lewman

Based on the screenplay by Tim Hill

Random House  **New York**

1

In the clear, sparkling waters of the southern Pacific Ocean lies Bikini Atoll.

"Atoll?" you ask. "What in the deep blue sea is an atoll?"

An atoll is a ring of islands formed by coral. In the case of Bikini Atoll, twenty-three beautiful little islands surround a shallow lagoon.

But our story doesn't take place on any of those twenty-three islands. Instead, our tale unfolds deep below the surface of the water in a wonderful undersea town called Bikini Bottom. The hero of our saga is SpongeBob SquarePants, a porous, four-cornered fellow who never met a stranger who didn't soon become a friend. And friends are what this story's all about. . . .

○ ○ ⊘

Let's begin at the very beginning. Many years ago, when SpongeBob was just a young sponge, his parents drove him to Camp Coral, a delightful summer camp where young ocean dwellers could do all sorts of fun things—dive off docks, paddle canoes, and sing songs around a campfire. (Yes, underwater. Don't ask how they built campfires underwater. They just did.)

The camp was run by friendly counselors who wore sweatshirts, and whistles around their necks. Most of the counselors had been happy campers at Camp Coral when they were little, and they liked it so much, they returned to work there when they were too big to be campers themselves.

SpongeBob's parents pulled their boat-car in front of the camp entrance, where a sign read CAMP CORAL. Excited, SpongeBob jumped out.

"Wooooo!" he whooped. "No way! Look at all the cool activities! Camping, canoeing, seahorseback riding, tug-of-war, whale watching . . ."

A large whale sipping coffee looked up from his newspaper at the little sponge with the big eyes staring at him. "Do you mind?" the whale asked, raising the newspaper in front of his face.

Unfazed, SpongeBob kept listing the cool activities. "Oyster hopping, juggling, and even shrink-wrap soccer!" He was vibrating with excitement and enthusiasm!

SpongeBob's dad watched his son bounce in place and smiled, remembering his own days at the camp. "Good ol' Camp Coral," he mused. "If you're lucky, son, you'll come home with two of life's greatest gifts: friends and memories."

"And every germ in the Seven Seas," SpongeBob's mom added nervously, handing her son his suitcase and toiletry bag. She hadn't gone to summer camp when she was little, and she'd heard camps weren't always perfectly clean. "Don't forget to take your vitamins, brush your teeth, and change your underpants."

"Okay, Mom," SpongeBob promised. "I won't!"

She handed him a big jar of vitamins and a toothbrush designed especially for his two front teeth. "And don't forget to flush your pores, dear." SpongeBob's mom took out a set of bellows and poked one end into a hole on the side of his head. She squeezed the handles together and water shot out of his other holes. *FWOOSH!*

"Okay, Mom," he said, taking the bellows from her. "I won't. Bye, Mom and Dad!"

Mrs. SquarePants felt a little teary as she watched her son run into the camp with his luggage. Mr. SquarePants got a lump in his throat. They squeezed hands. Their baby boy was growing up—spending time away from home!

But little SpongeBob didn't feel sad at all. He was TOTALLY excited to be at summer camp! He couldn't wait to paddle a canoe. To play tug-of-war. To try his hand at oyster hopping.

Mostly, he was excited about making new friends!

SpongeBob didn't waste any time. He ran right up to a boy fish. "Hi. I'm SpongeBob."

Before the boy fish could even answer, SpongeBob dashed over to a girl fish. "Hello, my name is SpongeBob."

He sprinted up to another camper. "Howdy, I'm SpongeBob."

He spotted a nearby counselor. "Nice to meet you," he said. "My name is SpongeBob."

By the lake, he hurried over to the members of the Camp Coral rowing team and introduced himself to every single rower. "Hi, I'm SpongeBob. Hi, I'm SpongeBob. Hi, I'm SpongeBob." He gave each of them a friendly wave as he moved down the line.

While the young sponge was busy trying to meet every person at summer camp, a big, expensive boat-car pulled up to Camp Coral's entrance. A serious-looking youngster named Squidward got out with his sleek bags. He closed the door, looked back, and said, "Bye, Mom."

Squidward's mother was in the driver's seat, talking on her shell phone. "Uh-huh," she said. "Uh-huh. Oh, one second." She looked toward her son. "Have fun at school, dear."

"Summer camp, Mom," Squidward corrected her.

Squidward's mom kept talking. "Your father would've loved to see you off, but he's, umm . . . busy." The person on the phone must have thought she was addressing them, because she added, "Oh, no. I'm talking to someone else."

Without giving her son a hug or a kiss, she roared away in the big boat-car, still talking on her phone. Squidward sighed and carried his luggage into Camp Coral.

SpongeBob was already deep into the camp, still introducing himself to people. "Hi, I'm SpongeBob. Hi, I'm SpongeBob. Hi, I'm SpongeBob. . . ."

Then he heard something he hadn't expected to hear at such a happy place as good ol' Camp Coral. Could it possibly be . . .

. . . someone crying?

2

SpongeBob followed the sound, which led him past the edge of the camp. Finally, he spotted a young pink sea star sitting slumped on a rock all by himself, crying.

SpongeBob put on his friendliest face and walked up to the sea star. "Hi. My name is—"

But before he could say it, the sea star cried louder. "Waaaaahhh!"

SpongeBob tried again. "Hi. My name—"

"WAAAAAAH!" the sea star wailed, even louder. Tears shot out of his eyes so forcefully, they knocked SpongeBob over. He got up and approached the young sea star once again.

"Hello, my name is SpongeBob. What's your name?"

"I'm Pa . . . Pa . . . Pa . . . trick," the sea star managed to say between sobs. Then he went back into full crying mode. "BWAAAAAAAAAH!"

"Why are you crying, Pa-pa-pa-trick?" SpongeBob asked.

"I'm . . . homesick!" Patrick explained, sobbing and wailing, tears streaming down his face and puddling around his feet.

SpongeBob felt sorry for Patrick. No wonder he'd been crying so much!

"Well, that's a pretty good reason," SpongeBob admitted. "Must be pretty hard when you don't know anybody, huh?"

"Yeah," Patrick agreed. He sobbed. "Pretty hard." He sobbed again.

SpongeBob sat on the rock next to Patrick. "Maybe all you need is a friend."

"WAAAAAH! I don't have any friends!" Patrick bawled.

SpongeBob grinned. "Well, you've got one now!"

"Really?" Patrick asked, sniffling and wiping the tears from his eyes. He looked around. "Who is it?"

"It's me!" SpongeBob said.

"Do you mean it?" Patrick asked, amazed that someone who had just met him, and had never seen him do anything but cry, was willing to be his friend.

"Of course!" SpongeBob said. "Things go better with friends! Two are better than one!"

From then on, SpongeBob and Patrick were the best of buddies. (And Patrick explained that his name was Patrick, not Pa-pa-pa-trick.) They went everywhere together, and did all kinds of fun camp activities. . . .

Near the lake, they found some big boulders to climb on. Laughing and shouting to each other, they scrambled up to the top. From there they could see the whole camp.

They paddled down a river in a canoe. Mrs. Puff rode in the back of the boat, teaching them how to steer. They didn't listen well, because soon they guided the canoe right over the edge of a waterfall. *SPLOOSH!*

Wearing helmets for safety, the pals zoomed down a zip line together. They couldn't believe how fast they were flying along! When they got to the end, they jumped off and ran back to ride it again right away.

They joined their fellow campers in target practice, shooting arrows at bull's-eyes with bows. SpongeBob impressed everyone when he shot a whole bunch of arrows out of his pores at once! They sailed straight toward the targets. *THUNK! THUNK! THUNK! THUNK!* Patrick was proud to be friends with such an incredible archer!

At lunch, Patrick popped up and surprised SpongeBob, who shot milk out of his nose. They both laughed really hard.

In the evening, they sat around a fire with the other campers, roasting marshmallows on sticks. The toasted treats smelled delicious, and tasted even better.

The next day, SpongeBob and Patrick swung on seaweed vines, pretending they were lords of the jungle. Then . . . *WHAM!* They slammed right into the side of a hill. But they were okay! Laughing, they got up and swung back the other way.

The friends explored a dark cave, which turned out to be the home of a giant cave monster. Luckily, he was a giant cave monster who had no interest in eating sponges or sea stars, so they got away safely.

On the beach, they shaped a TV out of sand and pretended to watch it. They were so convincing that other campers sat down to see what was on.

Patrick and SpongeBob borrowed a camera. They held it out at arm's length and took a selfie. Then they stared at the picture, watching it develop. Two friends! Together!

Once, when SpongeBob walked into the bathroom, Patrick started to follow, but SpongeBob stopped him. "Uh, Patrick, some things go better without a friend."

"Like what?" Patrick asked, puzzled.

SpongeBob closed the door to the bathroom.

"Ohhhh," Patrick said, finally getting it.

Just past the edge of Camp Coral lay beautiful kelp fields full of jellyfish. SpongeBob, Patrick, and the other campers loved going there with nets. They occasionally managed to catch a jellyfish, but they always let it go.

Waving his net frantically, SpongeBob chased a jellyfish toward his new friend. "Coming your way, Patrick!"

"Way ahead of you, buddy!" Patrick said

confidently. He swung his net at the jellyfish—but missed by a mile. The jellyfish gave Patrick a little sting. *ZAP!* Patrick made a face, then giggled. It didn't hurt . . . much.

Just then, a voice called out, "Woo-hoo! Hey, y'all critters of the sea! Look out beloooowwwww!"

3

SpongeBob and Patrick looked up toward the voice and saw something very unusual: a strange creature floating down, using a giant jellyfish as a parachute. Though the creature was new to Patrick and SpongeBob, anyone on land would instantly recognize her as a young squirrel—wearing a spacesuit with a glass-domed helmet. She carried a clipboard in one gloved paw.

When her feet touched the ocean floor, she let go of the jellyfish's tentacles. SpongeBob and Patrick ran over to greet her.

"Hello!" Patrick called. "Who are you?"

"Why, I'm Sandy Cheeks from Texas!" the squirrel announced.

"Hi, Sandy!" SpongeBob said. "I'm SpongeBob, and this is Patrick!"

"Pleased to meet ya!" Sandy replied.

17

SpongeBob looked closer at Sandy's interesting outfit. "Does everybody wear spacesuits in Texas?"

Sandy chuckled. "They do if they want to visit you underwater critters! We all breathe air on the surface!"

"Oh, right, air," Patrick said, nodding, as if he understood Sandy perfectly. "What's air?"

Sandy explained with a shrug, "It's just our way of synthesizing oxygen, same as you do with water."

Patrick stood there blankly.

SpongeBob was impressed with Sandy's explanation. "Whoa," he said. "Are you a scientist?"

Sandy giggled. "Nope, I'm a sixth grader. I like to observe stuff and then write it down and tell the whole class my findings!"

That sounded like a scientist to SpongeBob. "So," he said slowly, "you *could* be a scientist someday."

That made Sandy laugh. "Ha, ha, ha! You're a hoot, little dude!"

"Why not?" SpongeBob asked. "I think you'd make a great scientist, Sandy!"

Sandy shook her head in disbelief. "I'd be just as likely to live down here in a glass dome with a tree in it!" That thought made her laugh again.

SpongeBob grinned. "You never know!"

They both laughed. SpongeBob gave Sandy a friendly little punch. She gave him a friendly little punch back. He punched her just a tiny bit harder. She punched him back again. Giggling, they headed off with Patrick.

○ ○ ○

That night, the counselors at Camp Coral invited all the campers to participate in a talent show. After everyone who wanted to perform had done their act, the other campers would vote on which was the most entertaining. Whoever got the most votes would win the coveted Campy Award!

Larry, a young lobster who loved lifting weights, stood at the center of the camp's stage playing his accordion. At the end of the number, he demonstrated his awesome strength by ripping the accordion in half. *RRRRRIP!* The campers applauded. They liked Larry's act—especially the surprise ending.

As Larry walked off the stage, Mrs. Puff came out. She was the show's emcee.

"Thank you, Larry," she said into the microphone.

"You'll go far. Remember, people, *somebody* has to take home this year's Campy Award for most talented performer, so don't forget to vote!"

The campers in the audience nodded, holding up their ballots to show Mrs. Puff that they hadn't forgotten.

Backstage, SpongeBob and Patrick were getting ready to perform their act. They'd worked up a song, so they were warming up their voices.

"*La-la-la-la-la-la-la!*" SpongeBob sang.

"*Mi-mi-mi-mi-mi-mi-mi,*" Patrick warbled.

Squidward arrived just then, carrying a black case. "Greetings, Camp Coral pal-sies," he said. "I'm Squidward!"

"Hello, Squidward!" SpongeBob said. "I'm SpongeBob!"

"And I'm Patrick," Patrick added.

"Are you performing in the talent show?" SpongeBob asked.

"You betcha!" Squidward said confidently, opening the mysterious case. He removed a musical instrument. "My parents didn't spend good money on my clarinet lessons not to have me walk away with the Campy Award. That sucker is mine!"

To demonstrate how effective his expensive lessons had been, Squidward blew into the clarinet. It made a peeping sound. Patrick and SpongeBob were impressed.

"Whoa," Patrick said. "He's a pro."

On the stage, Mrs. Puff introduced the next contestant. "And now a special performance by Squidward."

"Well, good luck," Squidward said as he headed out. "To me! Haw, haw, haw!"

Squidward strode onto the stage. SpongeBob and Patrick hurried into the audience to watch.

"We gotta see this!" said SpongeBob.

Carrying his clarinet, Squidward crossed to the center of the stage and addressed the audience. "I would now like to perform 'Tentacles of Despair.' By me, Squidward Tentacles. And please save your applause until after the performance."

For a moment, Squidward stood still. Then he raised the instrument to his mouth and started blowing. There was a long squeak that shattered into a series of snarls and shrieks. The other campers looked dumbfounded. They'd never heard anything like Squidward's playing before.

Mrs. Puff sensed that the audience had heard enough. She lifted the needle off the record, and the music stopped. "Thank you, Squidward," she said. "Just lovely. So memorable."

SpongeBob and Patrick jumped up and down excitedly in their seats. "Yay, Squidward!" they cheered. "Nailed it! Bravo! Bravo!"

Squidward bowed. "Thank you. Thank you. Thank you. Thank you. Vote for me!" After several more bows, he leapt offstage.

Mrs. Puff looked at her list. "And now our next act . . . SpongeBob and Patrick!"

The pals looked at each other. "Come on! Let's go!" They ran from the audience around to the backstage area, ready to sing their hearts out.

Mrs. Puff spoke into the microphone. "Patrick and SpongeBob will be performing a duet called"— she consulted her notes—" 'Aka Waka Maka Mia.' "

A curtain opened, revealing SpongeBob and Patrick. They launched right into their song, dancing as well.

"Let me tell you about a puffer fish!" SpongeBob sang.

"Okay," Patrick said.

"A puffer fish with a dream," SpongeBob sang.

"Wow," Patrick said.

"He wanted to be bigger than life," SpongeBob sang, still dancing.

"Whoa," Patrick said, also dancing.

"Bigger than the sea," SpongeBob sang, flinging his arms open wide.

"That's kinda big," Patrick said.

"So he bought a pair of shorts . . . ," SpongeBob sang, acting it out.

"They were kinda tight," Patrick added.

"And protein bars to eat . . . ," sang SpongeBob.

"Yummy," Patrick said, rubbing his tummy.

"With a brand-new pair of running shoes!" SpongeBob sang.

"Um, puffers don't have feet," Patrick objected.

"Whatever, Patrick," SpongeBob said.

"Check this!" Patrick told the audience.

"Come on, Patrick!" SpongeBob cried.

They turned to face each other and did an elaborate hand-clapping routine. *CLAP-CLAP-CLAP-CLAP, CLAPPITY-CLAP-CLAP!*

"That's the stuff!" Patrick shouted.

"You got it!" SpongeBob yelled.

"Aka! Waka! Maka! Mia!" they sang together.

"Spent a lot of clams on his muscles, and . . . ," SpongeBob sang.

"Cha-ching!" Patrick exclaimed.

". . . *all day at the gym, hanging out with the heavyweights,*" SpongeBob continued.

"*But he was still slim,*" Patrick sang.

"*So he ate and he pumped and he did his sets until he threw up,*" SpongeBob sang, acting as though he were eating and lifting weights and barfing.

"Ughh," Patrick said, looking disgusted.

"*With his insides out, he sucked it in,*" SpongeBob sang.

"*That's when he blew up!*" they sang together.

Sticking a bellows into one of SpongeBob's pores, Patrick inflated his friend. *PUMP! PUMP! PUMP! PUMP!*

"*And grew,*" they sang. "*And grew. And grew. And grew. And grew. And grew. And grew. And grew. And grew. Grew, grew, grew, grew, grew, grew, grew, grewwwwwwww!*"

When SpongeBob had grown to a truly enormous size, Patrick yanked out the pump. *HISSSSS!* SpongeBob deflated, shooting around the audience like a balloon losing air. *ZOOM!* Campers ducked as SpongeBob rocketed straight toward their heads.

"Whoopsie!" Patrick cried.

When SpongeBob had lost all his extra air, he

ended up in the mouth of an audience member, who immediately spat him out.

"PA-TOOEY!"

SpongeBob landed on his feet, back onstage. "Ta-da!" he cried, flinging his arms open again. Patrick joined him in a final pose.

Silence.

"Haw, haw!" Squidward howled. "Terrible! The Campy is mine!"

A few minutes later, Mrs. Puff walked onstage with an envelope. Squidward quickly made his way there, sure she was about to announce his name as the winner of the Campy Award.

"The tally is in," she said. "And the Campy goes to . . ."

Reaching for the award, Squidward said, "Thank you. I'll take that."

". . . SpongeBob and Patrick!" Mrs. Puff declared.

"What? I—I—I . . . Huh?" Squidward stammered.

The audience went wild, bursting into applause, whistles, and cheers.

"Whaaat? No! PREPOSTEROUS!" Squidward screamed.

The audience gasped, shocked by Squidward's outburst.

"This isn't happening!" Squidward wailed. "Noooooo! Mommmmyyy!" He ran off the stage and away from the show, crying. SpongeBob and Patrick looked at each other, worried about their fellow camper.

○ ○ ○

In the hut where he slept every night, Squidward sat miserably on his bunk, sulking and moping. Patrick and SpongeBob peeked through the door.

"Squidward!" SpongeBob said cheerfully. "Just the Camp Coral buddy we wanted to see!"

"Go away!" Squidward snapped.

But they didn't go away. They went right into the hut and over to Squidward.

"Patrick and I were, um, talking to one of the counselors, and guess what?" SpongeBob said. "There was a big mistake."

"Uh-huh," Patrick confirmed.

"*You* actually won the Campy Award!" SpongeBob said.

"That's right," Patrick said. "Yep!"

"I did?" Squidward asked.

"By a landslide," SpongeBob said. He nudged Patrick, who handed Squidward the award.

"Hmm," Squidward said. "So weird they would have miscounted like that. But I guess . . ."

"Yay!" SpongeBob cheered. "Nice work, Squidward!"

"No one deserves it more," Patrick said. "Hands down."

"Wow!" Squidward said, turning the award around in his hands. "I really did it!"

While Squidward was concentrating on the Campy Award, SpongeBob winked at Patrick, who gave him a quick thumbs-up.

When SpongeBob was hungry the next day, he headed straight to Krabs Kantina. It was run by a friendly chef named Mr. Krabs in a sunken tugboat with a serving window. When SpongeBob got there, a bunch of campers were already lined up, waiting for some delicious grub. Running around participating in camp activities all day was hungry work!

At the front of the line, SpongeBob greeted Mr. Krabs, who was dressed in a chef's hat and an apron with food stains on it.

"Hello, Mr. Krabs!"

"Hello there, PlungerBlobby!" Mr. Krabs said, taking SpongeBob's tray.

"Mmm, close enough," SpongeBob said.

"How about a couple of Krabby Patties?" Mr. Krabs suggested.

"Gee, thanks, Mr. Krabs," SpongeBob said. "Those patties sure are tasty."

Mr. Krabs winked. "It's all in me secret formula."

"You should open up your own restaurant someday," SpongeBob said. "You could make a lot of money!"

Mr. Krabs smiled. "Oh, nay, lad. I'm a man of modest ambition. In the future, I doubt I'll care too much for money." He gazed off, thinking about the future, the word "money" echoing in his mind. He saw a vision of himself—older, in his own restaurant, standing at the cash register, ringing it over and over, saying, "Money! Money! Money!"

"Money! Money!" Young Mr. Krabs said, piling more Krabby Patties on SpongeBob's plate without even realizing it.

"Mr. Krabs . . . ," SpongeBob said.

"Money!" Mr. Krabs repeated.

"Mr. Krabs!" SpongeBob said sharply.

The chef snapped out of his momentary trance. "Oh! Sorry," he said. "Don't know what got into me there. Er, enjoy your patties, lad. For free . . ." He handed SpongeBob his tray, piled high with patties, through the window. SpongeBob grabbed the tray with both hands and walked away happily, eager to devour the succulent sandwiches with golden buns.

Patrick was next in line. "I'll take five—" he started to say.

"Be right back," Mr. Krabs interrupted. *SLAM!* He slid a metal covering over Krabs Kantina. When he raised it again, there was a sign that read ONE QUARTER PATTY—$1.50.

"Here ye are," Mr. Krabs said to Patrick. "One quarter patty with cheese." He quickly sliced away three quarters of Patrick's Krabby Patty.

"Wait!" Patrick protested. "That's it? What about my fries?"

"And one order of fries," Mr. Krabs said cheerfully. He took a single fry and snapped it into several pieces, which he dropped onto Patrick's plate. "Now pay up!"

○ ○ ○

As SpongeBob strolled away from Krabs Kantina, looking for a good spot to sit and enjoy his Krabby Patties, he heard a voice say, "Hello there."

He looked around but saw no one.

"To the left," the voice said. "Lower . . ."

He looked down and saw a small one-eyed, dark green creature standing next to a tiny food cart.

"That's it!" the creature said. "Hi! I'm Plankton! Welcome to my Chum Mobile! How about a nice Chummy Nugget with some Chumbucha?"

SpongeBob made an apologetic face. "Sorry, Plankton, but I just loaded up on Krabby Patties at Krabs Kantina."

"Of course you did." Plankton sighed. "Just like every other kid in this mudhole. What's that Krabs got that I ain't got, huh?"

SpongeBob thought about Plankton's question. "It's probably his secret formula for Krabby Patties."

"Secret formula?" Plankton asked.

"Sure," SpongeBob said, nodding. Then he got a brilliant idea. "Why don't you ask to borrow it? Mr. Krabs is very generous!" He tipped his tray a little, showing Plankton the big pile of Krabby Patties Mr. Krabs had given him for free.

"Say," Plankton said, brightening, "that's a good idea! I'm going to do exactly as you suggest! Bye, now!" He closed up his food cart, hopped into a tiny car, and buzzed off toward Krabs Kantina.

Mr. Krabs was still at the window, serving food

to a young customer. "Enjoy yer meal, lad," he said to the boy.

"Hello there!" Plankton called out from way down on the ground.

Mr. Krabs looked around but didn't see who had spoken. "Heh?" said. Shrugging, he turned away from the ordering window and went back into his kitchen.

Plankton managed to climb onto the counter. "Here!" he called.

Mr. Krabs turned and saw Plankton.

"Hello, Chef Krabs," Plankton said in his friendliest voice. "My name is Plank—"

WHAM! Mr. Krabs flattened Plankton with the back of skillet.

"—ton," Plankton groaned.

"Vermin," Mr. Krabs mumbled, thinking Plankton was some kind of sea bug. He hung the skillet on a hook with Plankton still plastered to the back of it.

"Jerk!" Plankton growled. "If it takes the rest of my life, I'll get you back for this!"

○ ○ ○

Near the lake, SpongeBob had finally spotted a perfect place to sit down and enjoy his Krabby Patties. He was sitting on a log, about to take his first bite, when he heard something.

"Meow."

He looked over and saw a small snail staring up at him.

"Hello, little snail," SpongeBob said. He gave the snail some of his food. The creature sniffed it—*SNIFF! SNIFF!*—and then happily ate.

"What's your name?" SpongeBob asked.

"Meow."

"Gary, huh?" SpongeBob said.

"Meow."

"Well, hi, Gary," SpongeBob said, smiling. "Gary, do you want to be friends?"

"Meow."

"Me too!" SpongeBob agreed.

And that's how SpongeBob met Patrick, Sandy, Squidward, Mr. Krabs, Plankton, and Gary—all at Camp Coral. His father had been right: SpongeBob had made lots of friends and memories at camp. He was one lucky sponge!

6

Years later, in Bikini Bottom, a clam stood on the town sign, crowing as a new day began.

"COCK-A-DOODLE-DOO!"

In his pineapple house, SpongeBob was still sleeping, snoring away. Gary knew it was time to wake up. He climbed onto SpongeBob and said, "Meow."

SpongeBob kept on snoring.

Gary slid across SpongeBob's face, leaving a sticky trail of slime. SpongeBob woke up. "Oh, morning, Gary!" Then he felt something on his face. "Ew, snail trail! Yucky!" He wiped the line of slime and thought again. "But oddly soothing!"

The sun pouring in through the bedroom window caught SpongeBob's eye. He jumped out of bed, ran over to the window, and flung it open.

SpongeBob leaned out and called, "Good morning, Patrick!"

Patrick's rock house flipped open with its owner stuck to the bottom. "Good morning, SpongeBob!"

"Good morning, Patrick!" SpongeBob repeated.

"Goooooood moooooorning, SpongeBob!" Patrick said, enjoying drawing out his morning greeting.

SpongeBob thought that was a good idea. "Good moooooooorning, Patrick!"

"Goooooooood morniiiiiiiiiiing, SpongeBob!" Patrick yodeled.

Squidward's tiki-head house sat between SpongeBob's pineapple and Patrick's rock. Today he had made a point of getting up early so he could practice his clarinet in peace and quiet. But SpongeBob and Patrick's yelling was disturbing his peace, as usual. He growled, annoyed.

"Good morning, Paaaaaaaaaatrick!" SpongeBob called, experimenting some more.

Squidward considered sticking his head out the window to yell at his noisy neighbors, but then sighed and put his clarinet back in his mouth. What was the point of yelling when he'd done it a million times before?

SpongeBob bounded down the stairs to his kitchen and poured a couple bowls of food for himself and Gary. "Come on, Gary! Breakfast!"

Gary slid up to the bowl of snail food and sucked it down in one gulp. *BURRRP!*

"You're welcome!" SpongeBob said to his beloved pet.

Gary loved his snail food. He was so happy, he turned over, lying on his shell with his tummy up, offering his belly to SpongeBob.

"Aww!" SpongeBob said, reaching over to scratch his friend. "Who loves a belly scratch! I love you so much, Gary!"

"Meow," Gary said contentedly, savoring the attention.

On the wall of the kitchen, a ship's clock chimed. *BONG! BONG! BONG!*

"Uh-oh," SpongeBob said, looking up at the clock. "I'm late if I'm going to be early!" He always liked to be early for his job at the Krusty Krab. When you love your job as much as SpongeBob loved his, you want your workday to start as early as possible! He hurried to the front door.

"Meow!" Gary protested, not wanting SpongeBob to leave.

"Aww, don't worry, Gare-Bear," SpongeBob reassured Gary as he opened the door. "I'll be back before you can say 'Why did he cruelly abandon me like that?'" He laughed at his own silly joke.

WHAM! SpongeBob slammed his front door and rushed off to work.

Gary's eyes welled up. "Meow," he said sadly.

SpongeBob ran all the way to the Krusty Krab, chanting, "I'm ready! I'm ready! I'm ready! I'm ready!" He opened the front door and hurried inside. After quickly assembling a punch clock, he inserted his time card. *KA-CHUNK!* When he pulled it out of the clock, the card read I'M READY!

"La-la-la-la-la-la," SpongeBob sang happily to himself, heading into the kitchen.

Squidward walked into the restaurant. He was in a bad mood. "Another day, another migraine," he grumbled, plopping down behind the cash register. "At least I'll get a little peace and quiet before that—"

"Good morning, Squidward!" SpongeBob warbled, popping up right next to his coworker.

"GAH!" Squidward yelled, startled.

"And isn't this a lovely morning?" SpongeBob asked.

Squidward frowned, folded his arms, and turned his back on the enthusiastic little fry cook.

"Nope," he growled. "Not talking to you. And I'm especially not getting involved in any of your nonsense today. I always end up with the wrong end of the stick!"

"Okay, Squidward," SpongeBob said pleasantly as he started to walk away. Squidward let out a big sigh of relief.

"But you should know," SpongeBob added, "Old Gertrude's getting pretty finicky these days."

Old Gertrude? Squidward thought. *Am I supposed to know who that is? I know I should just ignore him, but . . .*

"Old Gertrude?" Squidward couldn't help asking. "Who the kelp is that?"

SpongeBob was shocked. "You've worked with her for years! She's the eight-burner grill in the kitchen."

Squidward rolled his eyes. "It never ends."

Ignoring Squidward's comment, SpongeBob

went into the kitchen to prep his beloved grill. As he worked, he described to Squidward what he was doing through the order window.

"Anyway," he said, "to fire her up, you've got to spark her flints manually and then jiggle her gas jets just a little. And then read her favorite story, 'The Little Griddle Who Could.'"

SpongeBob pulled out a well-worn book, turned to the page with a grease-splattered bookmark, and started to read in a soothing voice. "'Chapter Two. "But we're fresh from the freezer," said the patties, "and we're co-co-co-cold!"

"'"Don't worry! I'll get you nice and warm!" said the little griddle.'"

Out by the cash register, Squidward was annoyed by SpongeBob's chatter. He turned and stuck his head through the order window. "What did I just say?" he barked. "Don't involve me!"

And then . . . *KA-BOOOOOM!*

7

Old Gertrude had blown! A burst of flame shot across the kitchen. Squidward pulled his charred head back through the order window and fell over the counter.

SpongeBob peeked through the window. "What did you say, Squidward? Squidward?" He looked around but couldn't see his coworker. "Okay, Squidward, doesn't matter. I'll always be here anyway."

Facedown on the floor, Squidward muttered, "Unfortunately."

Mr. Krabs came out of his office, humming a happy sailor's sea chantey to himself. He spotted Squidward lying on the floor. "Squidward, stop loafing! There's work to be done around here." The boss strode briskly over to a ship bell attached to a wall and yanked its cord three times. *CLANG! CLANG! CLANG!*

"Attention, Krusty Krew!" he bellowed. "Hoist the main sail! Full speed ahead!"

Mr. Krabs crossed to the front door, flipped the sign from CLOSED to OPEN, and flung the doors open. A huge crowd of hungry customers surged into the restaurant, trampling him.

But Mr. Krabs didn't mind a bit. "Heh-heh-heh," he chuckled as he lay on the floor, flattened. "Never gets old."

Later that day, SpongeBob cloned himself into several SpongeBobs so he could do *all* the Krusty Krab jobs. One SpongeBob shouted, "ORDER UP! MOVE IT! LET'S GO!"

Piling Krabby Patties on a tray, another SpongeBob answered, "Aye, aye, chief!" Laughing, he ran off with the tray to serve the patties to waiting customers sitting at tables around the dining room.

The SpongeBob in the kitchen kept ringing a bell, announcing that another order was ready. The SpongeBobs in the dining room rushed from counter to table, delivering food at lightning speed. All the SpongeBobs were laughing.

"DI-YI-YI-YI-YI!"

"One for you!" said one SpongeBob.

"Enjoy your Krabby Patty!" said another.

"Enjoy!" said a third.

The SpongeBob in the kitchen rang the bell again. *DING! DING!* "Order up! C'mon, SpongeBob!"

One of the SpongeBobs in the dining room said, "Coming, Fry Cook SpongeBob!" and laughed. Another did the same thing.

Squidward sighed, exhausted with SpongeBob's antics.

The front doors opened and Sandy entered, wheeling a big crate on a cart. "Hiya, SpongeBob!" she called to all the SpongeBobs.

"Hi, Sandy!" they answered at the same time. Then they merged back into one SpongeBob. *BOINK! BOINK! BOINK! BOINK!*

Sandy looked out from behind the big crate. "Did you know that in the future, everything will be automated?" she asked. "I'm gonna see if Mr. Krabs wants to be an early adopter of my new technology!"

"Wait, what?" SpongeBob asked, alarmed. "You're going to replace me with a robot! Don't do it!"

Sandy chuckled. "No, silly," she reassured him.

"That's gonna happen anyway." She patted the crate. "This is something much more innovative and start-uppy!"

"Oh, phew!" SpongeBob said, relieved.

Sandy went into Mr. Krabs's office to make her presentation. Sitting behind his desk, Mr. Krabs said, "You have sixty seconds," and started a timer. He didn't much like presentations. Most of the time, they turned out to be sales pitches that would only cost him some of his precious money.

"Their name is Otto!" Sandy said, popping open the crate to reveal . . . a robot! "They're an automated restaurant owner."

Mr. Krabs seemed intrigued, but then a look of concern clouded his face. "Hmm, automated? Sounds expensive. Not interested."

But Sandy wasn't going to be put off so easily. She believed in her invention!

"Otto doesn't require a salary," she explained. "And they can make cold, heartless decisions—like firing people—because they don't have a heart!"

Mr. Krabs leaned forward, peering at the robot. "Ye don't say."

"You're fired," Otto said in their robotic voice.

"Amazing!" Mr. Krabs said, impressed.

"I love money," Otto said. "I love money."

Mr. Krabs, overcome with truly heartfelt emotion, got up and walked around his desk. "A cold, unfeeling mechanical robot after me own cold, unfeeling crustacean heart." He nodded decisively. "I'll take it, and nurture it, and I will love Otto like they was me own son."

Sandy was thrilled! "Yipppeeee! You're not going to regret this, Mr. Krabs!"

She skipped out of the office, leaving Otto behind. Mr. Krabs hugged the robot.

Otto looked at him blankly and said, "You're fired."

"I could listen to that all day!" Mr. Krabs said, laughing. "Ack-ack-ack-ack!"

While Mr. Krabs stood there laughing, Otto moved behind the desk and sat in the boss's chair.

"No, seriously," they said. "You're fired. Please clear out your desk. You have sixty seconds."

He started a timer.

Sixty seconds later, the back door of the Krusty Krab banged open and Mr. Krabs stomped through it, carrying Otto over his head.

"No, YOU'RE fired!" Mr. Krabs shouted.

"No, you're fired," Otto replied calmly.

"Yer fired, ye infernal machine!" Mr. Krabs insisted.

"No, you're fired," Otto repeated in their same measured voice.

Mr. Krabs tossed Otto up and booted them with his foot, launching the robot into the air and across the street. *WHUMP!* Otto landed in the Chum Bucket's trash bin.

Brushing his hands clean and giving a satisfied grunt, Mr. Krabs turned and went back into his restaurant to resume his duties as the proud non-fired boss and owner of the Krusty Krab.

◯ ◯ ◯

Inside the Chum Bucket, Plankton's computer wife, Karen, turned from the television to see what had caused the loud noise. Rolling on her wheels, she went out the door into a back alley. She was alarmed to see Otto—a fellow machine—discarded in the trash bin! She moved closer . . .

Otto's mechanical arms reached toward her.

Hearts fluttered across Karen's screen.

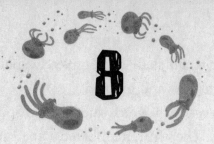

That evening at the Krusty Krab's closing time, Mr. Krabs stood at the door saying goodbye to the day's last customers.

"Thank ye! Thank ye! Come again when yer stomachs are empty and yer wallets are full!"

He counted the bills he held in his claw and chuckled with joy. "Heh-heh-heh-heh . . ." Then Mr. Krabs crossed the dining room to the cash register and tucked the money into the drawer. "Good night, Cashy," he said to the register. "I always sleep better on a full stomach, too."

He walked over to the kitchen door, opened it, and stuck his head in to yell at SpongeBob one last time before he left for the day. "SpongeBob! Be sure the kitchen's shipshape before ya head out, boy!"

SpongeBob answered in a French accent. "Oui, oui, Monsieur Boss Man Krabs! Once I am done here, zis kitchen shall be completely spotless!" He gave a little bow and giggled.

"Whatever," Mr. Krabs said, used to SpongeBob's silly antics. Then he remembered something. "Oh!" He pulled out a tray with a Krabby Patty on it. "I found this uneaten Krabby Patty on table six. You know what to do with it."

"Right away, Mr. K.," SpongeBob said, saluting. "I'll see that it's disposed of properly."

Mr. Krabs gasped in disbelief. "Who said anything about disposin' of? We'll sell it again tomorrow! On our Legacy Artisanal Vintage Throwback menu!" He and SpongeBob shared a laugh, and then Mr. Krabs left for the day.

"Good night!" SpongeBob called after his boss. He carefully placed the leftover Krabby Patty under a glass cover. "Huh!" he said to himself. "I better start cleaning!"

He had his work cut out for him. After a long, busy day, the Krusty Krab kitchen was a complete mess, with piles of dirty dishes and grease everywhere.

SpongeBob walked over to a bucket of soapy water, tossed a mop aside, and jumped in. *SPLASH!*

He scrubbed himself around the inside of the bucket. With soap bubbles rising out of his mouth, he proclaimed, "I'm ready!"

First, he slid across a counter covered in dirty dishes. By the time he reached the end of the counter, the dishes were sparkling clean!

Next, he splatted his soapy body against the wall and flopped across it—front, back, front, back—until the wall was wiped clean, too.

SpongeBob shot down to the floor and cleaned up every tiny drop of grime until it was perfectly clean. He stood to admire his work, then slipped off to fetch a sign that read CAUTION—WET FLOOR.

He went to the glistening grill and gave it a fond pat. "Well, good night, Gertrude!" He turned to the fryer. "Good night, fryer!"

He looked through the order window at the food under the glass cover. "Good night, patty!" He even said, "Good night, pickles!" to the pickle jar. He kissed the jar good night, shut off the lights, and left.

In the pickle jar, an eye opened and looked around to see if the coast was clear.

Plankton!

He'd disguised himself as a pickle, which worked well, since he was already green. He swam through the brine to the top of the jar wearing scuba gear and a utility backpack. He pushed open the jar's lid from the inside, climbed onto the rim, and took off his breathing mask and flippers.

"Good night, SpongeBob," he said in a low voice. "Hello, Krabby Patty."

The uneaten patty under the glass dome was sitting on the edge of the order counter. Plankton was sure that if he could just get his tiny hands on it, he could analyze the ingredients, revealing the secret formula behind the delicious Krabby Patty.

Plankton pressed a button on his utility backpack. *SPROING!* A spring popped out, launching Plankton through the air. He landed on the service counter, right next to the covered patty. "And now . . . ," he said, pressing another button on the backpack. *ZHOOMP!* A grappling hook fired out of the pack. Using an electronic remote control, Plankton guided the grabber claw on the grappling hook toward the handle on the glass dome lid. The claw closed around the handle, and . . . slipped off.

"Just gotta get it . . . ," Plankton said, concentrating. He guided the claw back to the dome's handle, and . . . got it!

"Ha, ha, ha!" he laughed triumphantly. "Yes!"

The claw released its grip. The dome fell back over the patty.

"Wait, wait, NO!" Plankton groaned. "NO! NO!"

He looked at his remote-control device. A message was blinking: INSERT COIN. "Stupid coin-operated . . . ," he grumbled as he dug out a coin and dropped it into a slot. Once again, the claw closed around the handle and lifted the cover. Sweating with effort, Plankton mumbled, "Come here. Come here. Oh . . ."

The claw held the cover suspended over the Krabby Patty.

"Bingo!" Plankton cried, moving toward the patty. He pulled a set of tweezers out of his backpack and eagerly plucked off a chunk of the Krabby Patty. He dropped the precious sample into his utility backpack. A screen on the backpack lit up: ANALYZING.

Plankton could hardly wait! "In just a few minutes," he said, barely able to contain his excitement, "the secret Krabby Patty formula will be mine!"

ZHIRRRR! His utility backpack printed out the secret formula!

"Yes!" Plankton uttered greedily. "Krabs's fast-food empire will fall, and I WILL RULE BIKINI BOTTOM AS ITS NEW SLOP KING!"

9

Plankton's evil laugh rang through the Krusty Krab. "AH-HA-HA-HA-HA-HA-HA!"

WHAM! SpongeBob slammed open the front door and turned on the lights. Startled, Plankton fell off the counter, releasing his hold on the secret formula.

"I KNEW IT!" SpongeBob said.

"AAAAAAAHHHHHH!" Plankton screamed. *SPLERSH!* He landed in a soapy puddle on the floor and slipped around the kitchen.

"I *knew* I left my keys in here!" SpongeBob said. "Silly me . . ."

Plankton kept slipping and sliding around the kitchen, unable to stand still and grab the secret formula. He reached for it, but it kept fluttering through the air, just out of his grasp.

SpongeBob looked around. "Huh," he said. "No

keys! That's weird. Where could they be?"

Plankton zipped past SpongeBob and ricocheted off the kitchen wall, screaming, "Ahhh!"

"Keys, keys, keys," SpongeBob muttered. "Where are my keys?"

As SpongeBob searched the kitchen, Plankton zoomed all over, barely escaping serious injury.

"Where are those keys?" SpongeBob repeated.

BONK! Plankton slammed into the mop bucket. Since it was on wheels, the impact sent it rolling across the floor and past the deep fryer, knocking both of its knobs into the "high" position. The grease in the fryer started to bubble. . . .

"Keys, where are you?" SpongeBob asked, still searching.

WHAP! Plankton crashed into a wall, knocking sharp knives loose. They plummeted straight toward him, and he dove out of the way at the last second. "AHHHH!"

He ran away from the knives, only to slip in another puddle and slide over to the CAUTION— WET FLOOR sign. The angled side of the sign acted like a ramp, launching Plankton into the air and toward the secret formula. He grabbed it!

Unfortunately, he landed in the potato slicer. *WHIRRR!* It turned on, pushing Plankton toward the deep fryer . . .

"Oh!" SpongeBob gasped. "My keys were in my pocket the whole time!" He held them up and jingled them, laughing. "Good night again, patty!"

He left without seeing the secret formula drift into the sizzling-hot fryer grease. The formula burst into flame, gone forever.

○ ○ ○

Later that night, Plankton lay in his tiny bed in the Chum Bucket, recovering from his injuries. He tossed and turned, mumbling, "Why? Why? Why?"

His wife, Karen, said, "You've been asking that question for twenty years, Plankton."

Plankton hopped out of bed. "And I still don't have the answer. No matter how ingenious my evil plans, success always slips through my fingers. Why?"

"It's pretty simple, Plankton," Karen said. But before she could give her husband the answer, he interrupted, continuing his tortured musing.

"When I was just a little lad, my parents taught me how to make chum," he said, pacing. Then he tripped, landing in a pile of chum. *PLOP!* Covered in chum, he continued to speculate on the cause of his failure. "They taught me how to cook with the chum. How to open my own restaurant. And the importance of keeping that restaurant growing, regardless of how much plotting and scheming it took. But no matter what brilliant plan I came up with to steal the Krabby Patty secret formula, someone always stopped me!"

"It's not who you think it is," Karen interjected.

"It's Krabs!" Plankton fumed.

"Nope," said Karen.

"I'm sure of it!" Plankton insisted. "It's Krabs!"

"No," Karen said. "Krabs is just the one inside your head. The one who always stops you, the one you should fear, is SpongeBob SquarePants!"

Plankton stopped dead in his tracks, stunned. "It is?"

"Absolutely. It's SpongeBob who always ruins your plans."

"No way," Plankton said. "But that's an interesting suggestion, Karen. Let me think a minute. . . ."

So Plankton stood there in the Chum Bucket, thinking. He remembered times when he'd tried to steal the secret Krabby Patty formula. . . .

He remembered a time when he'd tried to make off with the formula and gotten stuck on a balloon. Who was blowing up that balloon? SpongeBob! The sponge had plucked the formula out of Plankton's hands and locked it back in the vault.

Plankton remembered another time when he'd disguised himself as a Krabby Patty and scurried across the floor of the Krusty Krab. But SpongeBob was doing an Irish dance, and his foot stomped down, smashing Plankton and his disguise.

Another time, Plankton had succeeded in opening the secret formula's storage vault only to find SpongeBob inside with a birthday cake and a brightly colored banner that read HAPPY BIRTHDAY, PLANKTON!

His mind went back to the time when he'd put explosives around the Krusty Krab to blow it up, but when he pushed down on the detonator's plunger, he only succeeded in blowing up . . . a balloon! Which SpongeBob was sitting on!

He stopped thinking and turned to his computer

wife. "Karen, I just thought of something. All I have to do is get rid of SpongeBob, and the secret Krabby Patty formula is mine!"

Karen rolled her digitized eyes. "I don't know how you do it, Plankton," she said sarcastically.

"I amaze even myself sometimes," he said, smiling. "Now down to the evil plan. But first, a little orange juice to stimulate my gigantic brain."

He went into the Chum Bucket's kitchen and headed straight for the refrigerator. He opened the door and peered in. No orange juice.

"Karen!" he yelled. "Have you seen my—"

He turned and saw Otto chugging all of his orange juice right out of the bottle.

"What the—" Plankton said.

Karen rolled up behind him. "Oh. You found Otto!"

"Otto?" Plankton asked.

"So cute!" Karen gushed.

"What's up, bro?" Otto asked, offering the bottle of orange juice. "Want a swig?" The robot burped loudly.

"Uh, no thanks," Plankton said.

"You're fired," Otto replied.

10

Many miles away, in the palace of King Poseidon, ruler of the Seven Seas, the king's chancellor (called Chancellor) was hurrying through a long, ornate hall. Old paintings of former kings and queens hung on the walls.

Chancellor paid the paintings no mind. He'd seen them before. And right now, he was being called by the king.

"Chancellor! CHANCELLOR!" The king expected his closest advisor to come running any time his ruler called for him.

Chancellor pushed through a pair of double doors into a gaudy room, where the king did whatever he could to look his very best. At this moment, Poseidon was sitting in front of a large mirror with a golden frame, admiring himself.

"You sent for me, sire?" Chancellor asked, puffing a bit from running.

"Chancellor," Poseidon said proudly, without taking his eyes off his own reflection, "look at me. Three thousand years old, and check out my skin. It's like a baby's butt!"

"Ageless, Sire, ageless," Chancellor agreed.

"I owe it to my subjects to look fabulous, don't you think?" Poseidon asked.

"There are other obligations, sire," Chancellor gently reminded him. "Like . . . ruling and stuff."

Poseidon ignored his comment. "Time may take its toll on other kings, but not me." He smirked. "Because I care. I care about my appearance, and I take pains to maintain it." Then he noticed something in the mirror and leaned forward. "Wait . . . is that a *wrinkle*?"

The king frantically snatched a small hand mirror off the counter in front of him to get a closer look. "It is! It *is* a wrinkle! Ahhhhh! I look like an old avocado that's been forgotten in the fridge! Nooooo! I'm ugly!"

Desperately searching through his skin-care products, he wailed, "Oh, no. Oh, no! Where is it?

The crawly thing with the round shell and the eyes! *Where is it?*"

Chancellor stepped toward King Poseidon and held out a tray. On it was a very scared sea snail.

"Here you are, Sire," he said. "Your . . . snail."

Poseidon snatched the snail off the tray. "Oh, thank you! This mollusk has the rejuvenating power of a thousand facials!"

"Meow!" said the frightened snail.

The king rubbed the snail's underbelly against his face. But the snail left no trail of slime! "Is it empty?" Poseidon cried. He shook the snail like a bottle.

"Meow!" the snail protested.

"Take it away!" the king commanded.

A tiger fish rushed up and took the snail away. She opened a tube, placed the snail inside, and . . . *THUNK!* The snail was sucked down the tube.

The snail landed in a dark dungeon. Looking around in horror, the creature saw it was filled with sickly, dried-out snails!

Back up in the king's dressing room, Poseidon ordered, "Bring me another snail at once!"

Chancellor yelled to the tiger fish, "Another snail

for His Highness!" The tiger fish ran in, whispered something in Chancellor's ear, and handed him a tray with a shell on it.

"Uh, here you are, sire," Chancellor said, holding the tray toward the king. "Your . . . snail."

"Thank you," Poseidon snapped impatiently. "That took too long." He grabbed the shell off the tray and held it to his face. "YEOW!" he yelped. He pulled the shell away from his face, leaving a hermit crab pinching his cheek. "This isn't a snail! It's a hermit crab!" He yanked the crab off.

"Home-wrecker," the hermit crab said accusingly, before scurrying off.

"I've executed people for less!" Poseidon called after the crab.

Chancellor decided to come clean. "Okay," he said, taking a deep breath. "Full disclosure: we are out of snails. In fact, the entire snail population has been depleted."

King Poseidon looked puzzled. "By . . . ?" He raised his trident threateningly, ready to deal harshly with whoever had depleted the snail population.

Chancellor and the tiger fish exchanged a nervous look. They both knew it was King Poseidon himself, with his mania for using the snails' slime as a facial cream, who had wiped out all the snails. But Chancellor doubted the monarch wanted to hear that.

"By a . . . fluke," Chancellor said.

"A fluke?" Poseidon said, confused.

"Yes," Chancellor affirmed, nodding his head vigorously. "A fish very much like a flounder, Your Grace."

"I know what a fluke is!" Poseidon roared. He tossed his trident aside. "Chancellor, for the love of Hermes, my kingdom for a snail!" He considered what he'd just said. "No, *half* my kingdom for a snail! Wait, no—a boon. I'll grant a boon to whoever shall bring me a snail!"

Chancellor pulled out some parchment and a quill pen. "I'll draw up the decree, sire."

Not long after King Poseidon's call for a new snail, Plankton walked down the street in Bikini Bottom, mumbling to himself.

"*Pfff.* Karen, what an ingrate. Otto, Shmotto. I'll show ya who's cute. Run them through with a can opener. *Zing!* How would ya like *that,* robot punk?"

He noticed a royal page posting something on a pole. Then the page jumped into a seahorse-drawn carriage and sped away.

"What's this?" Plankton said.

He hurried over to the pole and started reading. "'A royal decree from King Poseidon'? 'To all citizens of the sea. The king requires a snail at once.' Blah, blah, blah, 'skin care,' blah, blah, blah, 'a boon is offered'? Poseidon—what a prima donna."

Plankton started to walk away, but then something occurred to him. He turned around, hurried back to the decree, and ripped it off the pole. "Wait a minute! A snail? No, it's too perfect! Too diabolical! Ha, ha, ha, HA, HA, HA!" he laughed maniacally.

○ ○ ○

SpongeBob walked in the front door of his house. "Gary, I'm home!"

Gary was usually right by the front door to greet him, but now he was nowhere to be seen. SpongeBob looked around for his beloved pet snail.

"Gare-Bear? Hey, where are you, buddy?"

He searched the living room. No Gary.

"Gary?" he called again.

SpongeBob reached into Gary's carpeted, multilevel sleeping space. There was nothing inside but snail sludge. "Gary?"

"You must be in the—" He pulled the cover off Gary's litter box. Snail-less. "Nope."

He opened a cabinet. Nothing. "Gary?"

SpongeBob frantically searched every inch of his pineapple house. "Gary! Gary? Gary? Gary! Where's Gary? Garrrrrrry!"

In the art room, Squidward had set up his easel

and was painting another self-portrait. This one showed him painting a self-portrait. He stopped painting for a moment and studied the picture, carefully considering his next brushstroke. He walked all around the easel, thinking.

SpongeBob suddenly popped up outside his window. "SQUIDWARD!" he yelled. "GARY'S MISSING!"

"Gah!" Squidward cried. Startled, his pushed his head through his painting. Then he pulled it out and pointed to the big hole where the picture of his face used to be. "SpongeBob, look what you did! Go away!"

SpongeBob's eyes welled up with tears. "Oh, I'm sorry, Squidward. That really is some of your best work."

○ ○ ○

Inside her treedome, Sandy was working on her garden when she heard SpongeBob knock on the glass. *BONK! BONK! BONK! BONK!*

"Sandy?" he called. "Sandy! Yo, Sandy. Sandy?"

"Grab a shovel, SpongeBob!" Sandy called back. "It's planting season for tubers. You got yer beets, and yer taters, and yer carrots . . ."

SpongeBob ran in through the treedome's airlock, quickly donning a water helmet. "Sandy, have you seen Gary?"

"Nope," Sandy said. "Besides, I wouldn't want to see a snail in my vegetable garden. Although technically, Gary's a sea snail, so it might be okay—"

"Sandy, this is urgent!" SpongeBob explained.

"Gotcha," Sandy said. "It's just, I'm a little busy. Can we do this later?"

"Oh," SpongeBob said. "Sure . . ."

"And don't worry about Gary," she reassured him. "I'm sure he'll turn up!" She grabbed a turnip and held it out. "Turn *up* . . . get it?"

But SpongeBob was already gone, intent on continuing his search for Gary. Sandy looked concerned for a moment, then turned back to her garden.

○ ○ ○

In his office, Mr. Krabs was enjoying watching the money-counting machine flip through bills on his desk. *WHIRRRR!*

"Now, *that's* the kind of robot I can get behind—one that counts money!" he said, chuckling.

SpongeBob ran in, out of breath. "Mr. Krabs! Have you seen Gary? He's—"

But Mr. Krabs cut him off. "Not now, SpongeBob. I'm in the middle of fanning the flames of me insatiable avarice! Go, baby, go, baby, go, go, go!"

SpongeBob's lower lip quivered.

◯ ◯ ◯

SpongeBob searched for Gary everywhere he could think of. He shinnied up a palm tree and looked through its fronds. He peered through his binoculars. He checked Jellyfish Fields. He even dug through the sand at Mussel Beach. No Gary.

As he searched, SpongeBob remembered lots of good times with Gary. Taking a bubble bath. Eating at a restaurant. Watching the sunset. Opening presents on Christmas morning.

Would he ever get to do those fun things with his pet snail again?

◯ ◯ ◯

While SpongeBob was searching all over Bikini Bottom, a carriage arrived at King Poseidon's palace. Royal pages rushed Gary inside, delivering him to Chancellor, who placed the snail in a jeweled case and hurried him into the king's dressing chamber.

Gary looked up and saw Poseidon's face looming over his.

"Hello, precious miracle of youth," the king said.

"Meow," Gary answered uncertainly.

○ ○ ○

Patrick opened the front door to SpongeBob's house and stepped in. "Hey, SpongeBob! I looked high and low for Gary and I found a sock!"

He held up an old sock.

Behind him, outside, a voice said, "Gimme that."

A fish wearing only one sock entered the house and snatched the sock out of Patrick's hand. As he turned and left, he growled, "Who takes a sock?"

Patrick looked around for SpongeBob. He spotted him lying flat on the floor surrounded by Gary's squeaky toys, staring up at the ceiling with his eyes full of tears.

"SpongeBob?" Patrick asked, worried about his friend.

12

"**O**h, Patrick," SpongeBob sobbed, still lying on the floor. "If something were to happen to Gary, I—well, I don't know what I'd do."

"Hey, maybe he left a clue!" Patrick suggested. He took a step to start searching for one, but tripped over one of Gary's toys and landed facedown in Gary's litter box. *SHWOMPF!* He lifted his head and spotted a piece of paper in the box. "Look!" he cried. "A clue!"

SpongeBob jumped up, ran over to the litter box, and snatched the piece of paper. He saw that it was a royal decree, and started reading. It didn't take him long to put two and two together. "Gary's been snail-napped!" he gasped. "And taken to the Lost City of Atlantic City!"

Patrick lifted himself out of the litter box,

spitting litter out of his mouth. *PTOOEY!* "Really?" he finally managed to say. "That's awesome! Now we know where he is!"

SpongeBob pulled a book called *The Nimrod's Guide to Lost Cities* off the shelf. He quickly flipped to the chapter on the Lost City of Atlantic City. "It's not really that awesome," SpongeBob warned his friend. "Listen to this: 'Made famous by the glitzy palace Poseidon calls home, the Lost City of Atlantic City is a scary, vice-ridden cesspool of moral depravity.'"

"Wow," Patrick marveled. "All that and it's lost, too?"

SpongeBob read on. "'King Poseidon has proved to be a whimsical tyrant, known for executing his subjects by beheading them in a flamboyant floor-show extravaganza. Our advice for those traveling here is . . . don't.'" He gulped. Sweat beaded on his face. "This King Poseidon sounds like a tough customer."

"Oh, yeah," Patrick agreed. "Tough."

SpongeBob straightened, shaking off his fear. "So what? This is about friends. And friends don't let friends become somebody else's face cream."

"Not what friends do!" Patrick said.

"So what if it's dangerous and scary?" SpongeBob said bravely.

"So what?" Patrick echoed.

"What is stopping me right now from going there, rescuing Gary, and standing up to this King Poseidon, huh?" SpongeBob said in his most confident voice.

"I don't know!" Patrick admitted.

"Well, I do!" SpongeBob declared.

"What is it?" Patrick asked.

SpongeBob sighed, looking defeated. "I don't have the . . . courage." He started to cry so hard that the stream of tears jetting out of his eyes launched him into the air and onto the ground. "Oh, Gary."

"Tartar sauce!" Patrick disagreed. "What's the next best thing to courage?"

"Resolve?"

"No."

"Fortitude?"

"Nah."

"Commitment?"

"Nope."

"Wherewithal?"

"Mm-mm."

"Bravery?"

"No."

"Valor?"

"What?" Patrick asked, not sure what that was.

"Grit?" SpongeBob guessed.

"Nope."

"Heroism?"

"Uh-uh."

"Gallantry?"

"Nah."

"Moxie?"

Patrick was tired of this guessing game. "A buddy!" he said. "A wingman."

"A wingman?" SpongeBob asked, not sure he'd heard that term before.

"Friends don't let friends go on dangerous quests to get back their snails alone!" Patrick said determinedly.

"Really, Patrick?" SpongeBob said. "You'd go with me?"

"Yeah," Patrick confirmed, nodding. "Right behind ya!"

They wasted no time. SpongeBob and Patrick marched resolutely out the front door.

"Okeydokey," SpongeBob said. "Now—let's drill down on the plan. Pat, you're in charge of transportation. Just remember, I don't drive and you don't have a car."

"Oh," Patrick said, stumped by this challenging situation.

Luckily, at that very moment a boat-car rolled up. Otto was driving, and Plankton was perched on the hood.

"Beep-beep!" said Plankton.

SpongeBob and Patrick stared at the robot-driven vehicle.

"Hey, boys!" Plankton said in his friendliest voice. "Don't know if you have any use for this ol' thing—if you're going on any trips or journeys or quests or rescue missions. But if you are, Otto is your ticket!"

"Otto!" SpongeBob and Patrick said, impressed by Sandy's invention.

"Just tell old Otto where you want to go and

they will take you there," Plankton explained.

"It is my pleasure to serve you," Otto said. "You're fired."

"Cool!" Patrick enthused. "A self-driving boat!"

"Thanks, Plankton!" SpongeBob said warmly. "You're the best!" He and Patrick hopped in the backseat.

"I know, I know," Plankton said immodestly as he waved at them. "Bye-bye."

"Otto, find Gary!" Patrick yelled. But Otto didn't understand that command, so they just drove the boat in circles until the vehicle ran into an old anchor. *CLUNK!*

"No, Patrick," SpongeBob said. "You gotta be more specific. Otto, find Gary the *snail*!"

More circles, ending in another *CLUNK*.

"Here, let me try," Plankton offered. "Otto, take them to the Lost City of Atlantic City and don't ever come back!" When SpongeBob and Patrick looked confused by the last part, Plankton explained, "Never hurts to exaggerate a little."

"It is my pleasure to serve you," Otto said in their robotic voice. The boat-car shot off like a rocket! *VROOOM!*

"WAA-HOOOOOOO!" SpongeBob and Patrick whooped.

"Bon voyage, boys!" Plankton called after them, waving.

As he watched the vehicle zip out of sight, Plankton chuckled, pleased to have gotten rid of SpongeBob and Otto in one brilliant stroke.

"I'm ready. I'm ready," he said to himself, imitating SpongeBob. "They're dead."

13

As Otto drove them along a winding road along the bottom of the ocean, Patrick turned to SpongeBob, pumped about their adventure. "This is gonna be like one of those buddy movies and *we're* the buddies!"

SpongeBob looked doubtful. "Not sure that really applies, Patrick."

"Why not?" Patrick asked. "We're two dudes setting out with a common goal. We'll argue about something dumb, fight, and break up, only to come back together when we realize neither could do it without the other. It's simple yet magical."

Still not convinced, SpongeBob said, "Yeah, well, it feels more to me like the journey of a singular hero who, against all odds, triumphs over adversity."

Patrick folded his arms across his chest. "Well,

I say buddy movie, and you say whatever that dumb thing was you just said."

"Really? Dumb thing?" SpongeBob said, getting mad. "I'm dumb? Oh, I *love* your sense of irony, Pat."

"Thank you," Patrick said. "I love my sense of ironing, too. Maybe if your head wasn't packed full of sand, *you* could have ironing!"

Now SpongeBob was really angry. "Well, better a head full of sand than a head full of rocks! Like yours!"

"That's *it*!" Patrick roared. He leaned forward to address Otto. "Stop the car!"

"Yeah, stop the car, Otto!" SpongeBob shouted.

RRRRRNNGRRRT! Otto slammed on the brakes and Patrick and SpongeBob flew out of the boat-car, screaming "WHOOOAAAA!"

They landed headfirst—SpongeBob in a pile of sand, and Patrick in a pile of rocks. *THWUMP!* They sat up, dazed.

"Sorry, Patrick," SpongeBob said. "Really, I shouldn't have said you have rocks in your head."

"I shouldn't have said your brain was made of sand," Patrick said. "That was mean and dumb."

"Okay, let's just forget it, huh?" SpongeBob suggested.

"Never happened!" Patrick agreed. They hugged. "What'd I say? Buddy movie!"

"We'll see!" SpongeBob said. As they walked back toward the boat-car, SpongeBob knocked sand out of his ear, and Patrick knocked rocks out of his.

Just when they were going to climb back into the vehicle . . . SCREECH. Otto pulled it forward a few feet and then stopped, messing with the passengers. The robot did this several more times until SpongeBob and Patrick finally managed to leap in.

They drove off toward the horizon, on their way to the Lost City of Atlantic City.

◯ ◯ ◯

Back in Bikini Bottom, a crowd had lined up inside the Krusty Krab, eager to place their orders. Alarmed by the long line, Mr. Krabs made his way past the customers.

"One at a time, people, one at a time," he said. "Heh-heh." When he reached the cash register, he asked, "Mr. Squidward, why aren't I seeing Krabby

Patties rolling out of the service window? Where's SpongeBob?"

Squidward shrugged. "How should I know? And frankly, you won't hear me complaining. Haw, haw."

Mr. Krabs headed straight for the kitchen and burst through the door. "SpongeBob! What's with yer lolligaggin', boy?"

SpongeBob wasn't there, of course. He was on his way to rescue Gary. But Mr. Krabs didn't know that. He looked high and low around the kitchen.

"SpongeBob? SpongeBob? Get out here this instant! That's a direct order! SpongeBob?" When he got no answer, he headed back out into the dining room.

"I don't get it," Mr. Krabs said, scratching his head. "He's NEVER missed a workday."

The crowd of customers was growing impatient. They started chanting, "KRAB-BY PAT-TY! KRAB-BY PAT-TY!"

One of the biggest customers angrily confronted Squidward. "Hey, where's my Krabby Patty?" he snarled, grabbing Squidward's arms. Squidward looked terrified.

"It's coming, sir, it's coming," Mr. Krabs assured the big guy. "Squidward! Get in that kitchen and try to whip up some Krabby Patties. I'll stay here and try to calm the crowd."

Happy to get away from the scary customer, Squidward ran into the kitchen. Sweating bullets, he faced Old Gertrude, the eight-burner griddle. "All right, Gertrude," he said, trying not to sound nervous. He opened the storybook. "Ahem. 'The Little Griddle Who—'"

KABOOM! Old Griddle exploded, flying up through the roof of the Krusty Krab and high into the sky, leaving Squidward with a blackened face.

Squidward stumbled back into the dining room. "Mr. Krabs, we've got a problem!"

"Squidward!" Mr. Krabs yelled.

Squidward was horrified to see two angry customers holding Krabs like a battering ram, slamming him into a support beam. *BANG!*

"Save . . . ," Mr. Krabs managed to say before they slammed him again. *BANG!* "YOURSELF!" The customers tossed him into the wall next to Squidward, who cowered in terror.

The crowd had become a mob. "RIOT! RIOT!" they chanted as they ripped tables off their stands. Horrified, Mr. Krabs and Squidward watched the riot rage in the Krusty Krab.

14

"**Q**uick!" Mr. Krabs hissed. "To the panic pantry!"

They ran away from the wall just as a table smashed against it, splintering to pieces. *CRASH!*

The panic pantry was a secret, secure room in the Krusty Krab where Mr. Krabs and his employees could hide in the event of a dangerous emergency. Squidward and Mr. Krabs huddled in the small room, shaking with terror.

"I never thought I'd see the day we'd have to use this room," Mr. Krabs said.

They could still make out the muffled sounds of angry customers rioting in the dining room. Mr. Krabs opened a tiny peephole and peered through. All he saw was a scene of destruction and devastation—furious Bikini Bottomites smashing tables, chairs, garbage cans, and anything else they could tear loose from the walls and the floor.

They threw tables. They ripped the boat that held the cash register from the floor and tossed it through the front window. *SMASH!* The cash register hit the ground with a loud *THUD,* and gave a pitiful little ring of its bell. *DING.*

"Oh, not me cash register!" Mr. Krabs wailed. "Oh, Cashy!" He began to sob, tears streaming down his face.

"Where is SpongeBob?" Squidward asked. "This is all his fault!"

○ ○ ○

At that moment, SpongeBob was snoozing, riding along in the boat-car driven by Otto. A bump in the road woke him up, and Patrick, too. They looked around and saw cacti lining what looked like a desert, not the bottom of the ocean. The water seemed to have disappeared!

"Where are we?" Patrick said sleepily.

"We must be dreaming!" SpongeBob said. It was the only explanation he could think of for the weird landscape around them.

Patrick laughed. "You amuse me, SpongeBob. Two people can't have the same dream, let alone be in that same dream at the same time. That would be philosophically untenable."

"Indeed," SpongeBob said, nodding slowly. "You make an interesting point."

"Wait," Patrick said. "We're talking like smart people. This *must* be a dream."

"Plus we're on the surface and we're breathing air," SpongeBob pointed out. "So, yeah."

Excited, Patrick took a deep breath and laughed. "Air! Ah-ha-ha! Ah-ha-ha!"

SpongeBob laughed, too. They drove over a rise, and an incredible view of the Painted Desert lay before them. They saw purple mesas, red clouds, and gray-blue sand. It was beautiful.

"Hey!" Patrick called out. "Town up ahead!"

They passed a sign that said GONER GULCH. In the near distance, they could see an old western town.

"'Goner Gulch,'" SpongeBob read aloud. "Huh. That's a funny name."

They soon reached the little town, stopping in front of a saloon. Patrick read the sign hanging out front: "'The Inferno Saloon. Ye Who Enter Here,

Abandon All Hope!' Guess that's another way of saying 'no public bathrooms.'"

SpongeBob and Patrick climbed out of the boat-car and looked around. A few tumbleweeds rolled by, but they didn't see any citizens.

"Hello?" SpongeBob shouted.

His voice echoed: *"Hello, hello, hello, hello."*

"Otto," SpongeBob said, a little nervously, "keep it close."

"Yeah, don't go anywhere," Patrick agreed.

"Go. Anywhere," Otto said. The robot hit the gas and roared away, leaving SpongeBob and Patrick in a cloud of dust. "It is my pleasure to serve!" they called as they sped off.

"Otto!" Patrick called after the robot.

"I don't think that robot's coming back," SpongeBob said.

A sagebrush tumbleweed rolled up behind them and knocked them down. They looked at the tumbleweed and saw it had a face!

"Hello," the tumbleweed said.

It spoke!

"Nyaaaaaaaah!" SpongeBob said, startled. "Who are you?"

"I am a simple tumbleweed," it answered. "Call me Sage."

"Sage," SpongeBob repeated.

"You're Sage," Patrick said. "Good name."

"Thanks," Sage said. "I'm made of sage, and I *am* a sage, so it works out pretty well."

"Wow," Patrick said, impressed.

"I am here to help you on your journey, SpongeBob," Sage explained. "But first you must accept a challenge."

SpongeBob stood up straight and put his fists on his hips. "I accept your challenge, Sage!"

"Well, no, hold on," Sage cautioned. "You should probably go through a period of agonizing self-doubt before you find inner strength and finally take up the challenge. I can help with that." He spat a coin out onto the ground. *PATOOEY! DING!*

"Eww," Patrick said, making a face. He thought spitting was gross. Unless he was the one spitting. Then it was fine.

"Take this Challenge Coin," Sage said.

"Challenge Coin!" SpongeBob and Patrick said. They liked the sound of that.

"It will give you courage whenever bravery is in

short supply," Sage said. "Which in your case we can assume is, like, all the time."

"Right!" SpongeBob bent over, picked up the coin, and held it up in the desert sunlight. "I have a Challenge Coin!"

"Okay, now pay close attention," Sage continued. "Your challenge lies behind these saloon doors."

"Let's go!" SpongeBob said. With his Challenge Coin, he felt ready to take on anything! He and Patrick walked toward the saloon.

"Wait, guys!" Sage called to them.

"Challenge Coin comin' through!" Patrick exclaimed.

"I didn't give you your challenge!" Sage protested.

But it was too late. SpongeBob and Patrick were already moving through the swinging wooden doors into the saloon.

Inside the Inferno Saloon, there wasn't a single customer or worker. A player piano was making music in the corner. On a table, they saw cards and poker chips, but no participants.

Suddenly, they heard voices! They couldn't see anyone, but they could hear lots of rowdy customers! Then, one by one, eerie figures magically materialized, laughing, drinking, and arguing. They were dressed in an odd mixture of pirate gear and cowboy clothing. But when SpongeBob and Patrick looked at their faces, they saw they were decaying zombies!

"WAAAAAAHHH!" SpongeBob and Patrick screamed. "Scary people!"

They leapt behind a barrel to hide, and Sage tumbled up next to them.

"Flesh-eating cowboy-pirate zombies, to be precise," he said.

"F-flesh-eating c-cowboy-p-pirate zombies, to be p-precise?" SpongeBob stammered. His knees were knocking together. So were Patrick's.

"This is your challenge," Sage explained. "Free these zombies of their earthly bonds and release their souls."

"If this weren't a dream, I'd be freaking out right now," Patrick said.

SpongeBob appreciated the reminder. "Oh, yeah! We are in a dream." He started singing a carefree little tune as he and Patrick came out from behind the barrel and crossed the room. "*La-la-la-la-la-la-*

la . . . Okay, everyone! We're here to release your imprisoned souls!"

KAA-KKROOOOM! Thunder crashed and lightning flashed!

"Wh-what was that?" SpongeBob asked.

15

On a steep mountain road, a team of wild, fire-breathing horses galloped furiously, pulling a black hearse with its curtains drawn. Their hooves thundered down the rocky pass. *CLOKA-BOOM! CLOKA-BOOM! CLOKA-BOOM! CLOKA-BOOM!*

Inside the Inferno Saloon, SpongeBob and Patrick looked worried. The cowboy-pirate zombies closed the curtains, as though they were preparing for the arrival of someone who liked rooms to be dark as night.

"El Diablo approaches!" one cowboy-pirate zombie rasped.

"We want to look lively!" said another.

"Make preparations!"

From what the cowboy-pirate zombies were saying about El Diablo, he did *not* sound like someone SpongeBob and Patrick wanted to meet. In fact, he sounded really scary.

The cowboy-pirate zombie at the piano started plunking out a different tune. One the others called the Gambler rapped about El Diablo's arrival. The other cowboy-pirate zombies danced along. The beat was so catchy that even SpongeBob and Patrick bounced to it, despite their fear about El Diablo showing up.

The wild horses pulled right up in front of the saloon, blasting fire out of their nostrils. The door of the black hearse swung open, and El Diablo stepped out. He was a zombie sea captain who carried a black lace umbrella. He slid the umbrella open and held it over his head to block the sun. Then he strode through the swinging doors of the saloon.

When they saw their leader, the cowboy-pirate zombies immediately stopped dancing. But El Diablo knew what they'd been doing.

"What did I tell you about dancing when I'm not here?" he growled in a low voice.

"But, boss," one cowboy-pirate zombie said, "it's Freestyle Friday!"

"SILENCE!" El Diablo roared.

He looked around the room and saw SpongeBob and Patrick standing on a table. He didn't know who they were, but he could instantly tell from their non-decaying faces that they weren't part of his fiendish crew.

"Bring the prisoners to my office," he commanded.

"Hey, yo, SpongeBob," the Gambler said to him quietly. "I gotta dip. Y'all got this." He slipped away.

"What was that guy talking about when he said 'prisoners'?" Patrick asked SpongeBob.

Before SpongeBob could answer, a cowboy-pirate zombie up on a balcony swung his sword and cut a rope. *CLANG!* A cage landed right over SpongeBob and Patrick, imprisoning them.

○ ○ ○

El Diablo's office was dark, with thick, black curtains covering the dusty windows. The villain sharpened a long blade as he spoke to his two prisoners in a small cage suspended over a desk.

"So, you dare to enter my ghost town, barge into my demons' lair, and tell my zombies you're going to free their souls, LIKE IT AIN'T NO THING?!"

"Well, uh, Mr. Diablo," SpongeBob said politely, "the good thing is, we're in a dream."

"A shared dream," Patrick added.

"Right, a shared dream," SpongeBob said, nodding. "So there's nothing to get all crazy about. It's not real."

"'Cause it's a *dream*," Patrick said, wanting to be absolutely clear.

"Who told you that?" El Diablo snorted. "The crazy bush guy? Well, what he should have told you was . . . IT'S NOT A DREAM!"

FWOOM! El Diablo shot fire out of his eyes, singeing SpongeBob and Patrick. They were impressed.

"He might be right, Patrick," SpongeBob admitted. "That felt pretty real."

"Yeah," Patrick agreed. "That really hurt."

Luckily, El Diablo's flame didn't just singe SpongeBob and Patrick—it burned the cage, too. The floor of the cage crumbled, and Patrick and SpongeBob fell through onto El Diablo's desk. *PLOP! PLOP!*

"Run!" Patrick shouted.

They scurried around the room with El Diablo right on their tails. He trapped SpongeBob and Patrick on the windowsill.

"Run, Patrick!" SpongeBob cried, pulling the Challenge Coin out of his pocket. He held it up to El Diablo, threatening him with it the way someone might hold a cross up to a vampire. "Foul demon, begone!"

"What the heck is that?" El Diablo scoffed, sneering at the coin.

"Huh?" SpongeBob said, surprised. He'd expected the zombie captain to cower in fear.

"What do I look like," El Diablo asked, "a parking meter?"

"But Sage said—" SpongeBob started to explain.

"Coin laundry is right down the street!" El Diablo said, laughing. "That's pathetic!" He stabbed his sharpened blade toward SpongeBob and Patrick, missing them by mere inches. But as he stabbed, his hand brushed against one of the curtains, pushing it open. A beam of sunlight streamed in, burning his hand! He dropped his knife and howled. "Owww! Get away from those curtains!"

"What, these curtains?" SpongeBob asked, taking one of them between his fingers.

"Oh, these are nice curtains," Patrick observed, feeling the material.

"They are!" SpongeBob agreed. "So soft . . ."

SpongeBob pulled the curtains open a little and sunlight poured in.

"YEEEEOOOWWW!" El Diablo screamed.

Patrick opened another pair of curtains. More sunlight drenched the room.

El Diablo screamed again. "YEEOOWW!"

"That's weird," Patrick said, staring at the curtains and not noticing El Diablo's reaction. He and SpongeBob both opened the curtains again.

"YEEEOWWW!" El Diablo screamed.

"The curtains are making a strange sound," SpongeBob observed. They opened and closed the curtains three more times. Each time, El Diablo screamed.

"I think the curtain rod needs some oil," Patrick decided.

"Once the rod goes," SpongeBob said, "you're better off getting a whole new set of curtains."

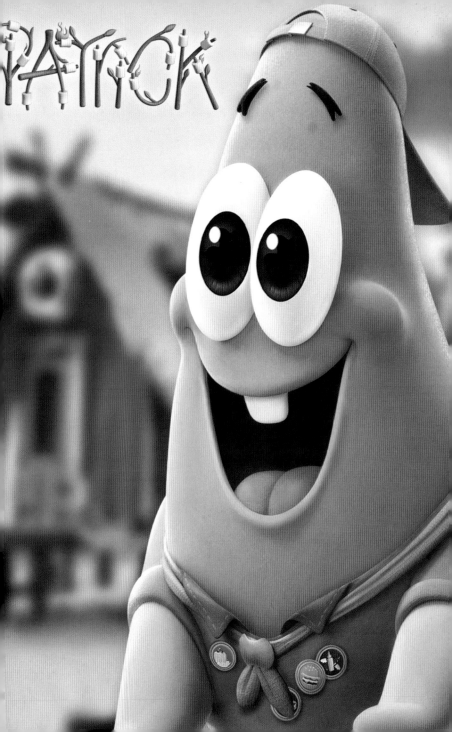

They pulled the curtains wide open. Sunlight streamed in, frying El Diablo to a smoldering crisp!

"Mr. Diablo," SpongeBob said as he turned away from the window, "I think your curtain rod might need a little . . . AAYYEEEH!"

He was shocked to see El Diablo reduced to a pile of ash!

"I guess too much sun *is* bad for you," Patrick said.

"Uh, Patrick, I think we should GET OUT OF HERE!" SpongeBob cried.

16

SpongeBob and Patrick hurried out of El Diablo's office and down the stairs. They slowed as they walked through the saloon, trying to act casual.

"Hey, everybody," SpongeBob said in his chillest voice. "El Diablo says he doesn't want to be disturbed."

"Yeah," Patrick added helpfully.

"Toodle-oo!" SpongeBob told the cowboy-pirate zombies.

"Buh-bye! See ya! Take care!" Patrick and SpongeBob said as they made their way toward the exit.

But before they could leave, all the cowboy-pirate zombies stood, raising their glasses in a toast.

"Adios, mateys!" one of them said.

"We're finally free!" added another.

"Huh?" SpongeBob said.

"Thanks, SpongeBob!" a third said gratefully.

"Later!" said a fourth.

All the cowboy-pirate zombies transformed into beings of pure, shining light and floated into the sky.

As he watched them go, SpongeBob got excited. "Patrick! Do you know what this means?"

"Definitely no ice cream here," Patrick said.

"No, silly," SpongeBob said. "We set the zombies free! That means we passed the challenge!"

As they celebrated their victory, they heard a gurgling sound coming from upstairs. Could it be . . . El Diablo?

They ran out through the swinging doors. Otto pulled up just then in the boat-car.

"Otto!" SpongeBob and Patrick called out.

"Howdy, pardners," Otto answered.

The two friends leapt into the boat-car.

"Let's get out of here!" SpongeBob cried.

At that moment, El Diablo, who had turned into a terrible ash monster, came roaring out of the saloon. SpongeBob and Patrick screamed. Otto floored it, and they sped away before El Diablo could reach them.

○ ○ ○

SpongeBob and Patrick woke up yelling. "Otto!" they yelped. "Faster! Go faster!"

"Wake up," Otto said calmly. "Your dream is fired."

"What?" SpongeBob said, shaking his head. "Oh, whew! See, Patrick? It must have been a dream!"

"More of a vision, really," Sage said. He was sitting next to them in the backseat of the boat-car.

"Sage?" SpongeBob said.

"Oh, hi, Sage," said Patrick.

"Hello," Sage answered.

"Are you real?" SpongeBob asked.

"As real as your desire to see that which you cannot," Sage said.

"Yeah, well, that which I cannot see is Gary, and I sure wish I could see him right now," SpongeBob said. "I gotta know what's happening!"

The tumbleweed almost seemed to nod. "This wish I grant you. Through the mystical fabric of the fourth dimension, you may now view what's happening at the same time as things are happening to you." A window appeared in the air right in front of SpongeBob and Patrick. "Behold the Window of Meanwhile," Sage said.

"The Window of Meanwhile?" Patrick asked. "What's it do?"

"It's like a video-on-demand service of parallel action," Sage explained, not all that clearly. "Have a look."

In the floating Window of Meanwhile, an image gradually came into focus.

"Uh, hey, Patrick," SpongeBob said. "Down in front."

The image in the mysterious window was . . . Gary! He meowed as King Poseidon wiped Gary's slime onto his face.

SpongeBob was horrified! "Gary!" he shouted. "We're coming to save you!"

"Okay, the Window of Meanwhile doesn't really work that way . . . ," Sage said.

"Hang in there, Gary!" SpongeBob called. "We got you!"

"Gary!" Patrick yelled.

"It's not a video-chat app like Skype or FaceTime

or anything . . . ," Sage said, getting a little exasperated.

But SpongeBob and Patrick just kept trying to talk to Gary, yelling at the floating window.

"Hello!"

"Over here!"

"Gary!"

"Run!"

"Get out of there!"

"Yeah, totally can't hear you," Sage said.

○ ○ ○

Plankton walked into the Krusty Krab to gloat over Mr. Krabs's loss of business since SpongeBob went missing.

"Hello, Eugene, old friend!" he sang out. "How's business? Tee-hee. Bad? Good! Well, that's a restaurant for you, eh? Feast or famine. Heh-heh."

Mr. Krabs just sat there, looking utterly defeated and glum.

"But I digress," Plankton said. "Why don't you be a good little loser and hand over the secret formula?"

Mr. Krabs sighed, and his breath blew the dust

off something in his hand: the secret formula. "Take it," he said. "It's yours."

Delighted, Plankton said, "Thank you, old buddy! Ha, ha, ha! Can I have these menu covers, too?"

"Take it all," Mr. Krabs said. "It doesn't matter anymore."

"Poor Kwabsie-wabsie!" Plankton said, pretending to feel sorry for his rival. "I hope you'll forgive a little old-fashioned gloating from a frenemy. Nyah, nyah, nyah-nyah, nyah! Heh-heh-heh. Loser! You!" Plankton made faces at Mr. Krabs, who just sighed again.

"Oh, Plankton," he said. "I wouldn't expect ye to understand, but somehow without SpongeBob, this whole thing—you, me, us—just doesn't make sense anymore."

Plankton frowned. "Wait, you're giving up? You can't do that! I've spent my entire career waiting for this moment, and you roll over like a harpooned whale? I won't let you rob me of my sweet vengeance!"

Mr. Krabs was already heading out of the Krusty Krab. "Give my regards to your lovely wife." Holding back tears, he sniffled and closed the door.

17

"**C**ongratulations," Otto said. "You have reached your destination."

SpongeBob and Patrick looked and saw, not too far off, the gleaming Lost City of Atlantic City. Soon they reached the city gates, which were set between two massive dolphin statues.

"The Lost City of Atlantic City!" SpongeBob said.

"It's pretty!" Patrick said, his eyes growing wider and wider at the sight.

And what a sight it was: a bustling, colorful, brightly lit metropolis full of rides and activities— all kinds of fun things to do and eat. It was like a giant theme park.

"Beware, young seekers," Sage warned when he saw SpongeBob and Patrick staring in wonder at the city's delights. "All is distortion. If you aren't careful, the Lost City will draw you into her fickle embrace, blind you with her dazzling distractions, and tempt you with her games of chance. Whatever you do, don't be led astray! Don't lose focus, and don't forget why you came here."

Climbing out of the car, Patrick and SpongeBob thought Sage's warning was completely unnecessary.

"Thanks, Sagemeister," Patrick said. "I think we got this."

"Yeah, Sage," SpongeBob said. "I mean, you've been pretty good up until now, but I love Gary more than anything in the whole world, and we came here to get him back. We are not about to lose our focus. Let's go, Patrick."

And so our two brave heroes walked through the gates into the city . . .

. . . and immediately lost their focus.

Their eyes popped even wider at all the amazing sights, spinning like wheels.

A candy salesman cried, "Cotton candy!"

An ice cream salesman yelled, "Ice cream!"

A churro salesman offered his goodies, too, really

rolling his *R*s: "CHURRRRRRROS!"

SpongeBob and Patrick were so excited by all the sweets, and the bright lights, and the wonderful smells, and the music playing everywhere, that they couldn't even speak in sentences. All they could muster were grunts and whoops.

They rode a roller coaster!

They ate pizza!

They drove bumper cars!

They ate ice cream!

They went to a medieval feast!

Eventually, SpongeBob and Patrick wandered into one of the many casinos, the Shipwreck Casino. They didn't understand gambling, but they liked all the flashing lights and ringing bells.

"Isn't it cool how they let you trade in your real money for these little plastic circles?" SpongeBob said, holding up a handful of poker chips.

"Casinos are magical," Patrick said.

They strolled over to a roulette table with a spinning wheel, which they found fascinating. Holding ice cream floats with straws, SpongeBob and Patrick stared at the spinning roulette wheel.

SpongeBob was tired of carrying the little plastic

circles he'd traded his money for. He asked the dealer at the roulette table, "Would you mind if I put these down, sir?"

"Place them wherever you like," the dealer said.

"Just put 'em on *L*," Patrick suggested.

SpongeBob looked at the table. "Patrick, that's not an *L*. That's a seven."

"Seven starts with an *L*?" Patrick said, looking surprised. "That's weird."

The dealer gave the roulette wheel a spin and tossed in a marble. SpongeBob and Patrick's eyes followed the ball around and around as it bounced in the spinning wheel. *CLINK! PLONK! PLUNK!* Finally, it came to rest.

"And . . . seven!" the dealer announced. He slid stacks of poker chips toward SpongeBob and Patrick.

"More plastic circles!" SpongeBob cried, thrilled.

When they saw the big stacks of chips SpongeBob and Patrick had won, a group of casino customers gathered around.

"Who are you guys?" SpongeBob asked.

"We're your entourage," one guy with a ponytail answered.

SpongeBob and Patrick weren't sure what an entourage was, but they always enjoyed making new friends. They led their entourage in a conga line, dancing out of the Shipwreck Casino and into another casino next door.

There they soon found the crappie table, where excited gamblers were betting on rolling dice.

"Place your bets!" the dealer said.

"Come on, seven!" Patrick yelled.

SpongeBob shot two dice out of his sponge holes onto the table. Covered in goo, they stuck to the side of the table. *SHPLORP!*

The dealer looked at the dice. "Lucky seven!" he announced. "Winner!"

SpongeBob, Patrick, and their entourage moved on to another casino and tried their hands at a game called baccarat.

"Seven! Seven! Seven!" Patrick chanted. And when he took a bathroom break, he kept chanting "Seven! Seven! Seven!" from the stall.

The two buddies and their entourage danced their way onto a gondola floating down a canal, singing and laughing.

At the Davy Jones Resort, SpongeBob and

Patrick surfed on an artificial wave in a giant pool, slurping down drinks with little umbrellas sticking out of them.

"Hey, Patrick!" SpongeBob called to his friend.

"What up, Spongey-Dog?" Patrick said.

"I lost all my money!" SpongeBob said cheerfully.

"Ha, ha!" Patrick laughed. "Me too!"

Riding the wave next to them, the entourage said, "Aww," and surfed away. Once SpongeBob and Patrick didn't have any money left, the hangers-on weren't interested in them anymore.

But losing their money and their entourage didn't stop Patrick and SpongeBob. They made their way to Club Tsunami, where a crowd cheered while the two pals did some break dancing to a pounding beat. From the sides of the club's stage, fireworks went off. *BOOM! POW!*

They danced and laughed long into the night. . . .

The next morning, an octopus with a dustpan in each tentacle cleaned litter and garbage off the sidewalk outside the dance club. Patrick slept on the sidewalk wearing a dented party hat. He had confetti on his shoulders, and cradled a plush carnival toy in his arms as he snored.

The octopus dumped garbage into a trash can with two feet sticking out, one of them missing a shoe. The feet belonged to SpongeBob, who tried to crawl out of the can. He tipped it over. *CRASH!* The sound made Patrick wake with a start.

"Party people!" he shouted. Then he looked around. "Oh. Where is everybody?"

SpongeBob coughed. *"Ack! Cack! Blak!* I feel like I swallowed a sea urchin," he said hoarsely.

"Me too," Patrick said. He coughed up a sea

urchin and spat it on the ground. "Hey, I *did* swallow a sea urchin."

"Well, well, well . . . ," said a familiar voice. Sage rolled up to them.

"Sagester!" SpongeBob croaked. "Good to see ya, pal!"

"Nice work, boys," Sage said sarcastically. "Way to take my pearls of wisdom and flush them down the toilet."

SpongeBob wondered what Sage was talking about. Then he remembered.

"Oh, no," he said. "Oh, wait. Did we?"

"Lose focus, like I told you not to?" Sage suggested.

"Not me," Patrick said.

Sage sighed. "Let me jangle your minds. You came here to get back something you lost, something you love."

Suddenly, SpongeBob and Patrick both *really* remembered. "Gary!" they cried out at the same time.

"Yeah, Gary," Sage said. "Seriously, it's hard enough being stuck in a tumbleweed—"

"Patrick, we gotta find Gary!" SpongeBob said.

"—but dealing with you two makes me want to light myself on fire," Sage complained.

"Sage! Buddy!" SpongeBob said urgently. "Can we please look into the Window of Meanwhile one more time to see where Gary is?"

Sage seemed annoyed by SpongeBob's request. "No! It's not an on-demand service!"

"Actually," Patrick pointed out, "you called it 'a video-on-demand service of parallel action.'"

Sage ignored this. "Fortunately for you, you woke up right here, on the steps of Poseidon's palace."

SpongeBob and Patrick whipped around and saw a sign over the entrance to the building in front of them: POSEIDON'S PALACE & CASINO. Without even saying goodbye to Sage, they ran inside, back on track to rescue Gary.

The palace's lobby was very fancy, overloaded with glittering crystal and decorations.

"Whoa!" they said when they saw it.

"Get a load of this place, Patrick," SpongeBob said, amazed.

A security guard tapped SpongeBob on the

shoulder. "Can I help you two bumblefish?"

SpongeBob turned around. "Yes, kind sir. We would like an audience with His Majesty, King Poseidon."

The guard began to snicker. "Hold on . . . ," he said, giggling. His laughter grew and grew until he was bent over, guffawing. He laughed so hard, he nearly passed out. Emergency nurses arrived, set him on a gurney, and gave him oxygen. A team of doctors crowded around the gurney, working to revive the guard.

"Patrick," SpongeBob whispered, "I think we'd better move along."

"I think so," Patrick agreed.

They started down a beautiful hallway, but guards followed them. "Hey, you two!" one of the them shouted. "Get back here!" SpongeBob and Patrick turned a corner and broke into a run. The guards pursued them.

Patrick and SpongeBob saw a door that said AQUA LOUNGE and they slipped inside. A bellboy rolled a food cart away, revealing the rest of the sign: PERFORMERS' ENTRANCE.

In a backstage dressing room, SpongeBob and Patrick found racks of costumes and shelves of props.

"Wow, look at this stuff!" Patrick exclaimed. He quickly donned a coat with a big fur collar and a derby with a long feather. Doing a little dance step, he asked SpongeBob, "So, tell me what you *chitty-cha-cha* think."

SpongeBob had disguised himself, too, putting on lots of makeup and a top hat. He answered in a Southern accent: "Well, c'mon! What do you thaink?"

"Impressive, sir," Patrick said, studying him.

"Then shall we, sir?" SpongeBob asked.

"Indubitably, sir," Patrick answered.

They did a couple of goofy dance steps until a stage manager poked his head in the dressing room. "Quick, you two! Get ready! You're on!"

"Huh?" SpongeBob and Patrick said. They'd just been messing around. They had no intention of going out onto the Aqua Lounge stage and performing.

But the stage manager was already pushing them

toward the stage. "Just get out there and knock 'em dead!"

"No, we're just—we're not—" they protested.

"And remember," the stage manager added, "Poseidon's in the audience."

"Poseidon?" SpongeBob asked.

Patrick grinned. "We *are* getting an audience with the king!"

SpongeBob and Patrick stumbled onto the stage, shoved from behind by the stage manager. They stood there in silence, staring out at the audience staring back at them.

They tried playing pat-a-cake, slapping their hands together. They ended by making fart sounds with their hands in their armpits. *PBBT! PBBT!*

Silence.

"Patrick," SpongeBob whispered. "Let's give 'em our old song from camp!"

" 'We'll Always Be True to You, Camp Coral'?" Patrick whispered back.

"No," SpongeBob whispered. " 'Aka Waka Maka Mia'!"

"Oh, right!" Patrick said, grinning.

They launched into the song they'd won the

Campy Award with all those years ago. They sang! They danced! They did pat-a-cakes! They bumped butts!

And they built to a big finish, striking a pose with their arms stretched wide open.

Silence.

But then . . . laughter! The audience was *roaring* with laughter!

And up in his box seat, so was King Poseidon. Laughing and applauding, the ruler shouted, "Bravo!" Patrick and SpongeBob spotted him.

But then the king caught a glimpse of himself in a mirror and gasped. "Laugh lines! Chancellor! Get me my—"

Before the king could even finish his command, Chancellor rushed over with Gary, who meowed. Poseidon took Gary and rubbed him against his face.

"Gary!" SpongeBob and Patrick cried. They jumped off the stage and leapt from table to table, making their way toward the king's balcony box.

"Gary, I'm coming, buddy!" SpongeBob shouted, hopping across the audience members' tables.

"Excuse me. Sorry. My bad." To reach Poseidon's box, Patrick stood on a lounge patron's head, and then SpongeBob stood on Patrick's head.

SpongeBob managed to peek over the railing of the balcony box. Poseidon looked alarmed, but SpongeBob spoke. "Hi there," he began. "Excuse me, King Poseidon, sire, but there's been a misunderstanding about Gary."

Poseidon seemed confused and offended. "Gary?"

"Gary!" SpongeBob repeated.

"Meow," Gary said.

"Gary?" Poseidon asked again, still not knowing who SpongeBob was talking about.

"The snail you're rubbing all over your face right now," SpongeBob explained.

King Poseidon looked at Gary. "Nonsense," he said. "This snail's name is Fred."

Now it was SpongeBob's turned to look confused. "Fred? You renamed Gary?"

"Fred," Poseidon said.

"Gary," SpongeBob said, reaching for his snail.

"Fred!"

"Gary!"

"FRED!"

"GARY!"

"FRED!"

"GARY!"

Throughout the argument over Gary's name, SpongeBob and Poseidon had a tug-of-war with Gary, pulling him back and forth. Finally, SpongeBob lost his grip and fell back down to the tables, taking Patrick and the lounge customer with him. *WHUMP!*

Poseidon pointed over the edge of the balcony at SpongeBob and Patrick. "SEIZE THEM!"

Guards quickly grabbed SpongeBob and Patrick.

"Gary! Gary!" SpongeBob called to his snail friend. "Gary loves me! And I love him!"

"Meow!" Gary agreed as the guards hauled SpongeBob and Patrick away.

***

Back in Bikini Bottom, Sandy sped up to SpongeBob's house on a rocket-powered sled. *ZOOM!* She knocked on the door, but no one answered. Letting herself in, she looked around and saw no sign of her friend.

"Hello?" she called out. "SpongeBob! Get yer

copilot goggles, dude, cause we're goin' sleddin'! SpongeBob? Hello?"

She looked in SpongeBob's shower. "SpongeBob?"

She looked in his refrigerator. "Hey, you in here?" *SPLAT!* An unrecognizable piece of food collapsed. "Whoa!" Sandy said, backing away.

She looked in his bedroom. "SpongeBob?"

A framed picture of herself and SpongeBob as children at Camp Coral sat on the dresser. She picked up the picture and studied it, remembering those happy days. Sandy wiped a tear from her eye, then got a determined look on her face.

○ ○ ○

In the Krusty Krab, Mr. Krabs glumly flipped menus into a wooden barrel. Squidward read a fan magazine about his favorite clarinetist, Kelpy G. Sandy burst in through the front door.

"All right," she barked. "What'd y'all do with SpongeBob?"

Squidward looked up from his magazine. "We don't know where he is, Sandy. He hasn't been here in days."

Sandy wasn't buying it. "Don't you play coy with me, cephalopod!" she snapped at Squidward. Then she turned to Mr. Krabs. "And you, arthropod! Start talkin'! Where is he? Tied up in the basement? Stuffed in your trunk?"

Mr. Krabs shook his head sadly. "Nay, I could never harm the lad. His absence has taught me that much. But I'm not talking about the money I'm losing with him gone. Well, maybe I'm talking about that a little. Okay, fifty percent talking about the money, and fifty percent I truly miss the boy."

"I hate to admit it," Squidward said, "but things just aren't the same without him."

"There's no denying it," Mr. Krabs agreed. "We need SpongeBob."

"Did anyone ever stop to think he might need *us*?" Sandy asked.

Right at that moment, a news report came on the TV. "Perch Perkins," said a reporter, "coming to you from the Lost City of Atlantic City." He stood right in front Poseidon's palace. Speaking into a microphone, he gestured to the ornate building behind him. "I'm standing outside Poseidon's

Palace and Casino, where two suspects have been taken into custody tonight after trying to attack the Royal Snail."

The screen showed mug shots of SpongeBob and Patrick, and a picture of Gary sitting on a beautiful silk cushion. Then a video of SpongeBob and Patrick performing "Aka Waka Maka Mia" started playing.

"The sponge and the sea star were impersonating a lounge act," the reporter continued, "when they made an attempt on Poseidon's prized mollusk."

The TV showed Poseidon rubbing Gary on his face.

"It's Gary!" Mr. Krabs, Sandy, and Squidward all cried.

"In a related story," Perch Perkins went on, "Poseidon's Palace and Casino presents a command performance, featuring the execution of the suspects in the Aqua Lounge, this Friday night."

Mr. Krabs jumped to his feet, outraged. "Execution of the suspects?" he sputtered. "What happened to habeas swordfish?"

"It's a fun-filled family event with opening act, Kelpy G!" Perch Perkins said cheerfully. "One performance only. Tickets still available."

"We gotta go help them!" Sandy said.

"We embark immediately!" Mr. Krabs agreed. "Mr. Squidward, are ye comin'?"

"Hah. Fat chance," Squidward said. Then he added, "Fat chance I'd miss a Kelpy G performance! I'm in."

"TO THE PATTYMOBILE!" Mr. Krabs bellowed.

20

In the Krusty Krab garage, Mr. Krabs yanked the cover off the Pattymobile, revealing an old boat-car shaped like a Krabby Patty.

"What, this old tub?" Squidward scoffed.

"Never judge a Pattymobile by its buns, Squidward," Sandy cautioned, hitting a button. *BRRRRROOOOM!* New jet turbine engines fired up. She hit another switch and the Pattymobile stretched until it was streamlined, like a supersonic submarine. Pickle wheels extended from the body and a row of tomatoes lined the cab. Two engines, shaped like ketchup and mustard bottles, hung on either side.

"Let's light this puppy!" Sandy said.

Squidward and Mr. Krabs jumped into the Pattymobile and Sandy hit the throttle. *VROOOOM!* It took off like a rocket!

"Mommmmyyyyyy!" Squidward cried, terrified. He, Mr. Krabs, and Sandy were flattened into their seats by the force of acceleration. Outside, the Pattymobile left a long, smoking trail of ketchup and mustard.

∅ ∅ ∅

In Poseidon's dark dungeon, SpongeBob slowly slid off a wooden stool in shock and despair.

Patrick looked over at him lying on the floor. "SpongeBob? Are you okay?"

"It's just that I failed, that's all," SpongeBob said, crying. "And I'll never see innocent little Gary again. Oh, my heart is BROKEN!"

"Aw, come on, now," Patrick said. "Buck up. It's not over yet, SpongeBob."

SpongeBob pulled himself to his feet. "It sure feels over," he sniffed. "And crappy."

"Just sayin' there's two sides to every coin," Patrick said.

"Oh, Patrick. What does a coin have to do with—" Then SpongeBob stopped. "Did you just say *coin?*"

"Huh? Me?" Patrick asked. "I don't think so."

"You did!" SpongeBob cried. "You said 'coin'!"

"Not remembering that exactly," Patrick said.

"The *Challenge Coin*!" SpongeBob said. "Of course! Don't you see, Patrick? We're saved!" But when he searched his pockets, he came up empty. "Patrick!" he cried, horrified. "It's gone!"

"Eh, I don't know," Patrick said. "Was the Challenge Coin really that useful?"

"Hey, wait a sec," SpongeBob said slowly. "I gave it to you, remember? For safekeeping."

"No," Patrick said.

"Come on," SpongeBob urged. "It was last night. We were at the crappie tables."

SpongeBob thought back to the night before. He pictured Patrick at the crappie table, wildly shouting, "C'mon, seven! C'mon, seven! C'mon, seven!"

"Place your bets," the dealer had said.

Patrick had casually flipped the Challenge Coin onto the square on the table marked "7."

SpongeBob remembered now. "You gambled away my Challenge Coin? You wrecked our entire mission with one stupid bet?"

"You need to remember what you said just *before*

126

that," Patrick said, now remembering the night himself. SpongeBob had wildly urged him to "Let 'er ride, Patrick! Let it ride!"

And Patrick had said, in a very reasonable voice, "But, SpongeBob, what if you need the Challenge Coin tomorrow to help you summon your courage?"

With his eyes flashing wildly, SpongeBob had said (at least in Patrick's memory), "Tomorrow is for WEENIES!" And then he'd laughed insanely.

"Well, it's tomorrow," Patrick said to SpongeBob in the dungeon. "And guess who's the weenie!" He stalked off and sulked in the corner of their cell.

SpongeBob fumed. "I. CAN'T. BELIEVE YOU!"

"Told you this was a buddy movie," Patrick reminded him.

"Hey, losers . . . ," said a voice outside the cell.

Sage rolled up and looked at SpongeBob and Patrick through the metal bars.

"Hey, Sage," Patrick said.

"Sage, glad you're here!" SpongeBob said, hurrying over to him. "Guess who gambled away my Challenge Coin?"

"Guess who blames everyone else for his troubles?" Patrick countered.

"Oh, yeah, coin-gambler-away-er," SpongeBob said accusingly.

"Blamer," Patrick said.

"Stupid breath!" SpongeBob name-called.

"Blame-gamer!" Patrick snapped.

"Okay," Sage interjected. "Did I mention that you are the *worst* epic heroes for whom I have ever been a spirit guide?"

SpongeBob thought about this. "Hmm. I think we went over that this morning?"

"I believe we did," Patrick said, nodding. "Yeah."

Sage took a deep breath and let it out slowly, trying to be patient with SpongeBob and Patrick. "The coin was just a symbol. The courage you seek is inside you, not in the coin. And it will come to you in your hour of need."

SpongeBob looked confused. "But isn't *this* my hour of need?"

"Oh, no," Sage said. "It gets much worse."

21

Then Sage rolled away.

"Bye!" he said.

SpongeBob looked at Patrick. "Worse?"

"Dude said *much* worse," Patrick corrected him.

A noise outside the palace drew them to the barred window of their cell. They peered out and saw letters being put on the building's marquee. "'Sponge and Star Execution Extravaganza'?" SpongeBob read. "Oh, that couldn't be for us." Then he realized, "It *is* for us, Patrick! We're gonna die!"

Chancellor and a prison guard arrived at their cell. "Prepare the prisoners!" Chancellor ordered. "Well, kids," he said to SpongeBob and Patrick, "it's your big moment to fry . . . er, I mean . . . shine!"

The guard opened the cell door and motioned with his spear. SpongeBob and Patrick came out and followed Chancellor down the hall. The guard was right behind them, pointing his spear at their backs.

"Please follow me to the Green Mile . . . uh, greenroom, I mean," Chancellor said. "Everyone says the show is going to be electrocuting . . . electrifying. So sorry. I keep accidentally mentioning methods of execution."

"It's cool," SpongeBob said, shrugging. "Don't lose your head over it."

"Or lethally inject yourself," Patrick added.

"Anyway," Chancellor said, "if it's any consolation, you're the hottest ticket in town."

They didn't react. The guard gave them a poke with the tip of his spear, and they let out a little halfhearted cheer.

"Yay . . ."

◠ ◠ ◠

Mr. Krabs, Sandy, and Squidward zoomed through a hyperloop in the Pattymobile, on their way to the Lost City of Atlantic City. *WHOOSH!*

"Mr. Krabs," Sandy asked, "what are we going to do when we get there?"

"I don't know," he admitted. "But maybe you two could kick in some gas money."

○ ○ ○

In the Aqua Lounge, a master of ceremonies walked onstage with a microphone and said, "Ladies and gentlefish, welcome to the greatest show underwater! Now, without delay, let's meet the contestants! In this corner, a sponge and a star, two of the ocean's most notorious criminals!"

As SpongeBob and Patrick were wheeled out and seated at a courtroom defense table, where a BOO! sign lit up.

The audience members were only too happy to oblige. "BOO!"

"And in this corner," the master of ceremonies continued, "representing His Majesty the King, Poseidon's very own . . . Chancellor!"

As Chancellor, wearing a powdered wig, was rolled in on a courtroom podium, an APPLAUSE sign glowed. Once again, the audience followed directions.

"Now," said the master of ceremonies, "put your hands together for the Duke of the Dirty Deed, the

Earl of Executions, that axe-wielding maniac . . . LEMONT!"

Lemont, a big lobster wearing a hood and carrying an axe, strode onstage. The audience *loved* Poseidon's executioner! They chanted, "LE-MONT! LE-MONT! LE-MONT!"

"Ladies and gentlemen," the master of ceremonies said, "now a moment of smooth jazz in memory of the soon-to-be-gone. I give you . . . Kelpy G!"

While Kelpy G serenaded the audience, SpongeBob leaned over and whispered to Patrick, "Oh, Patrick! I feel terrible! I dragged you into this whole mess."

"It's okay, SpongeBob," Patrick whispered back. "I made a plea deal with the prosecution." He winked at Chancellor, who winked back.

"Oh, that's good!" SpongeBob said. "Wait . . . you did what?"

"All I have to do is . . . uh . . . ," Patrick said, thinking hard. "Oh, yeah! Bring incriminating evidence against the defendant."

SpongeBob jumped up from his seat. "Patrick, *I'm* the defendant!"

"You are?" Patrick said, surprised. "Ohhhh . . ."

"Listen, Patrick," SpongeBob whispered. "I've got a different idea." He quietly told the plan to his friend, whose eyes got big. Patrick smiled and nodded.

From his balcony box, King Poseidon ordered, "Let the proceedings begin!"

Chancellor spoke from behind his podium. "Your Honor, I would like to enter into evidence one sea snail. Name? Fred." Guards brought Gary out and placed him on a small table.

"Meow!" he cried when he saw SpongeBob.

"Gary!" SpongeBob called.

Chancellor pointed an accusing finger at SpongeBob. "How dare you! That's about all I can say. How dare you come here to the sanctuary of our revered sovereign to steal what is most precious to him! To rob him of that which pumps his very life blood—his adorable good looks! HOW DARE YOU!"

The crowd gasped, impressed by Chancellor's speech.

"Guilty!" shouted Poseidon. The crowd cheered, calling out for Lemont the Executioner. But then the power went out! In the darkness, a hooked cane

133

yanked Chancellor away from the podium.

"Hold it!" said a voice.

FWOOM. A spotlight glared on, revealing Patrick standing behind the podium. "I have something to say," he announced solemnly. "Just two words: Challenge. Coin."

"Challenge Coin?" Poseidon said, baffled. "What is *that* supposed to mean?"

Patrick grinned. "I'm glad you asked, Mr. King-Guy. I will be glad to explain."

Chancellor pushed his way into the circle of light, right next to Patrick. "Stop! This is most irregular! You are one of the defendants! You can't just get up and start talking! This is a trial, not a talk show! Guards!"

The guards started to move toward Patrick, who held up a hand. "Just a moment," he said in his most grown-up voice. "I believe Mr. King-Dude asked me a question. If I do *not* answer the king, I'm disobeying his command, right?"

Chancellor hesitated and thought for a moment. "Well, I guess technically—"

Patrick turned to the audience. "Do *you* think I should answer the king's question?"

The audience cheered and clapped. They were pretty sure that saying you shouldn't answer the king's question could get you in serious trouble.

"Okay," Patrick said. "So that's settled. Now, Mr. Kingly-Person asked me what I meant when I said 'Challenge Coin.' You see, once upon a time, there was a sponge and a sea star in a scary little town called Goner Gulch. . . ."

Patrick told the story of how he and SpongeBob had gone to Goner Gulch and met Sage the tumbleweed, and received a Challenge Coin, and taken on El Diablo and his cowboy-pirate zombies. He told it all the way through, to the moment when he and SpongeBob had sped away from the ash monster El Diablo had changed into.

The audience listened to Patrick, spellbound. Even King Poseidon enjoyed Patrick's story. He'd never heard of cowboy-pirate zombies, or Challenge Coins, or talking tumbleweeds who offered wisdom and guidance.

"Quite a tale," he said when Patrick had finished.

"Thanks," Patrick said.

"But what has it got to do with trying to steal my snail?" King Poseidon asked.

"I don't know," Patrick said, shrugging. "Nothing."

Angered by Patrick wasting his time, the king scowled. But then he realized he was frowning, and that frowning put lines in his forehead. Wrinkles! He quickly reached for "Fred." But his snail disintegrated in his hand! It was a fake. A decoy!

"Huh?" Poseidon said, astonished. "My snail!"

During Patrick's story, SpongeBob had sneaked up into the king's balcony and swapped a decoy for Gary. As soon as he had his pet snail back, he'd slipped out of the Aqua Lounge, followed by Patrick.

King Poseidon realized he'd been fooled. "Halt!" he bellowed. "It's a trick! SEIZE THEM!"

22

Patrick and SpongeBob (carrying Gary in his arms) sprinted through the confusing hallways of Poseidon's huge palace. The guards chased them.

"Gary!" SpongeBob said joyfully. "You're with me now! I'll never let anyone take you again!"

"Meow!" Gary said gratefully.

"Let's go, Patrick!" SpongeBob urged. "Faster!"

But Patrick spotted a buffet table covered in delicious food. He stopped, out of breath, but he managed to gasp. "Wow," he said.

Running down the hall, SpongeBob looked back over his shoulder. "Patrick! What are you doing?"

"Free food . . . ," Patrick said, sounding as though he'd been hypnotized. He loaded up a bucket with food as the guards closed in on him. SpongeBob yanked him away just in time. They ran down the hallway, Patrick gnawing on a turkey leg.

Grease from Patrick's food dripped onto the floor. When the guards reached the puddle of grease, they slipped and fell. *WHAM!*

"Nice going, Patrick!" SpongeBob cheered as he looked back at the fallen guards.

"Yeah, that was my plan all along," Patrick claimed.

But the guards jumped right back up on their feet and took off, sliding down the hallway on their greasy boots as if they were skating on ice. They were coming at SpongeBob and Patrick even faster than before!

"They're gaining on us!" SpongeBob cried. "They're going to catch us!"

"Bummer," Patrick said.

But as they passed a side corridor, Mr. Krabs, Sandy, and Squidward zoomed into the hall in the supersonic Pattymobile! *VROOOM!*

"Mr. Krabs! Sandy! Squidward!" SpongeBob cried with delight. "How did *you* get here?"

"As ye can see, we traveled by Pattymobile," Mr. Krabs said. "But never mind that now. Just keep running, and leave those blasted guards to us!"

As SpongeBob and Patrick ran down the hallway,

Mr. Krabs spun the Pattymobile around so its trunk was facing the rapidly approaching guards. Sandy pressed a button on the dashboard, and the rear pickle wheels rose up so the Pattymobile was level with the guards' faces.

"Wait for it," Squidward said, twisting around in his seat to see. "Wait for it . . . NOW!"

Sandy punched another button on the Pattymobile's control panel. *SPLOOSH!* Ketchup and mustard blasted out of the nozzles on the sides of the vehicle, shooting through the air and right into the guards' eyes. *SPLAT! SPLAT! SPLORT! SPLOOP!*

"AHHH!" the guards howled. "It burns! Spicy!"

"Spicy mustard," Mr. Krabs chuckled. "Works every time."

Blinded by the condiments, the guards slammed into the walls of the corridor, knocking themselves out. They lay in a big pile on the floor.

"Nighty-night!" Squidward called to them, waving goodbye as Mr. Krabs lowered the back pickles, spun the Pattymobile around, and zipped down the hallway to pick up SpongeBob and Patrick.

"Thanks, Mr. Krabs! And Sandy! And

Squidward!" SpongeBob said as he climbed into the Pattymobile with Gary and Patrick. "How can I ever repay you?"

"Just come back to the Krusty Krab and whip up a fresh batch of Krabby Patties!" Mr. Krabs said.

"Will do!" SpongeBob agreed, laughing.

But as they drove toward a palace exit, Gary let out a loud "Meow!"

SpongeBob looked concerned. "What is it, Gary?"

"Meow! Meow, meow, meow!" Gary explained.

"Got it!" SpongeBob said. He turned to his friends. "Gary says there's a dungeon full of snails here. We've got to free them, too!"

"Really?" Squidward said. "I didn't sign up for this."

But Sandy said, "You got it, SpongeBob! Gary, show us the way!"

With Gary directing, they drove straight to the snail dungeon. Sandy used one of her scientific tools to open the lock on the door, and they flung it open. Hundreds of snails crawled out, delighted to be liberated!

"Woo-hoo!" SpongeBob whooped. "Crawl! Crawl! You're free!"

Mr. Krabs steered the Pattymobile toward the exit, followed by the stampede of freed snails. They zoomed away from the Lost City of Atlantic City, heading home to Bikini Bottom.

As they left the city, King Poseidon ran out of his palace, shaking his fist at them. "Come back here!" he commanded. "I'm not done punishing you! I need my SNAIL!"

In a way, he got his wish. As he shouted at the retreating Pattymobile, the stampede of snails swarmed all over him, knocking him to the ground and leaving him trampled as they moved on.

"Unnnghhh," he groaned.

◯ ◯ ◯

When SpongeBob, Gary, and their friends got back home, their little town sparkled under the sun and swayed in the warm, gentle currents.

And as his father had predicted, SpongeBob had gained new friends and memories from his adventure—a great treasure indeed!